BRITISH BLACK SHEEP

EVER AFTER
BOOK FIVE

LAUREN SMITH

For Kate and her loveable scamp, the bulldog Yogi who gave me so much joy when writing this book.

live like
there is no
Midnight

ONCE UPON A TIME...

A PRINCE LOST HIS WAY IN THE WOODS
UNTIL HE FOUND A PEASANT GIRL TO
SHOW HIM THE WAY HOME...

1

"Y**ou're not going to die."

Brie Honeyweather laughed at her friend's quip over the phone. If anyone could calm her down right now, it was Veronica.

"I know," Brie said with a sigh. "But it's been a while since I've taken one of these international flights. It's a little scary. That's all." She shifted on the blue leather chair in the gate area. Her flight was scheduled to board in half an hour and all around her the other travelers were stuffing snacks in carry-on bags and adjusting curved pillows around their necks.

"It'll be fine. Thad, Lyra, and I just landed this morning. We're on our way to Merryvale Court. We can't wait to see you."

Brie grinned as she hastily pulled her backpack out

of the way of a passenger stepping through the rows of chairs.

"I'm excited, too. I still can't believe you helped arrange all this. I mean, Christmas in an English country house? It's going to be a dream come true." Brie could already picture the snowy gardens, taste the Christmas pudding, and see a large tree shimmering in the great hall.

"I only got the ball rolling, Brie. When I sent your books to the Countess of Merryvale, she was so impressed. She was so taken with your writing that she called your publisher for her Christmas holiday book."

Brie blushed. She'd been a ghostwriter in Chicago for four years and loved writing the stories and biographies of famous people, but this project with the countess felt different. The countess called Brie three months ago and explained in a beautifully polished British accent that she wanted to write a Christmas tradition book detailing how the holidays were celebrated on grand British estates over the years. Brie had been hesitant until she'd realized that Merryvale was the location where her favorite Regency romance series had been filmed. Both Merryvale and the countess were legendary—to Brie at least, who'd poured over the garden maps and immersed herself in the architectural history of the grand manor house.

"So, you leave at 7:30 tonight and you arrive at 7 AM tomorrow in London? Are you staying in the airport all day tomorrow to wait for your flight to Manchester?" Veronica asked.

"Yeah. I have to. My flight from Heathrow to Manchester leaves around about six. Then I'll have a car take me to Merryvale tomorrow night." Brie glanced around at her fellow passengers in the gate area. "The flight is going to be packed."

"At least the countess is flying you first class."

"I *know*." Brie exclaimed. "I've never flown first class in my life."

"And overseas is the best. You get those little pod things to sleep in. It's so nice. Lyra and Thad stayed up all night watching movies, of course. Now he's exhausted."

"Thad?" Brie giggled.

"Yep," Veronica laughed. "Lyra never runs out of energy." Lyra was Veronica's six year old daughter from her first marriage. Four years after her husband died in a car accident, Veronica had met and married Thad.

"How does Thad know the Countess of Merryvale? I feel like I need to start taking notes." Brie was beginning to think she needed a notepad to jot down all the family members and the titles of her hosts.

"Thad did a few college summers at Cambridge

where he met Lady Merryvale's son. They're 'old school chums' as he says. Thad's friend called his mother and had her invite Thad, Lyra, and I for Christmas. She thought it was a great idea since she was having you fly over for a few days."

Brie dug around in her backpack for her laptop to take some notes. "Right." If she was going to write about Merryvale and its family she was going to need more details.

"Well, I should go. You'll be boarding soon...and I need to stop Thad from buying half the convenience store snacks for Lyra before we get back on the road."

"Good luck!" Brie chuckled and hung up.

A minute later, the flight attendant at the gate desk announced that special needs passengers and families with priority boarding were to line up. First class would be next. Brie took one last moment to people watch at the gate, creating little stories about them in her head. The older couple who were dressed expensively, perhaps an anniversary trip? The family of six with two exhausted parents and wrinkled clothes, a Christmas vacation?

And then she saw him...

Mr. Gorgeous-as-a-God. He had to be six foot two with a trim, muscled physique all poured into an expensive tailored business suit. He had a rolling attaché briefcase made of what looked to be brown Italian leather. His dark golden hair was long enough for a woman to run her fingers through and grip tightly if she wanted. And she wanted. She wanted to commit his features for later mental replay. It was a long flight, after all.

He had a chiseled look that made her want to trace his face with her fingertips and memorize all the hard angles from his jaw to the straight nose and proud chin. He had a cell phone out and was casually texting with one hand while holding the handle of his briefcase with the other. Such an ordinary everyday thing to do shouldn't have been attractive, but there was nothing more enticing than a man who looked like he meant serious business. Maybe it was because men like that could be so damn hot when they unleashed all that focus and intensity on a woman. Brie couldn't tear her eyes away from him. He was just so *gorgeous*.

Most people in the airport had that harried, frantic look or they appeared disgruntled and rumpled. But this man looked like he'd walked off one of those video billboards in the terminal that featured attractive men in Gucci or Armani suits.

"First class passengers group 1, please line up for boarding," the flight attendant announced.

A small collection of thirty people got up along with

Brie to jockey for position at the entrance of the gate. Brie winced as her backpack straps dug into her shoulders. She wished she could have put more items in her checked suitcase, but she needed to work during the flight. If she didn't stay busy, she would freak out.

Mr. Gorgeous was at the front of the line and he held out his phone, swiped his boarding pass and went straight onto the plane. The rest of the passengers ahead of her weren't as organized and most had to dig for their boarding passes. By the time Brie was at the attendant station, she had her pass out.

As she headed down the gangplank, her stomach knotted with nerves. Flying always made her anxious. She just repeated Veronica's words in her head over and over.

You won't die. Everything will be fine.

As she boarded the plane, she glanced around the first-class seats and scanned for 4D. It was a window seat.

A window seat next to Mr. Gorgeous.

No...No...No. She did not want to sit down next to this guy. Sure, he was *insanely* hot, but he was the very opposite of her type. Okay, that was a lie, he was totally her type, but she was refusing to have a type right now. She'd married too young and divorced too soon, and Brie was not about to make the mistake of falling in lust with someone like her ex ever again. And this guy was just like Preston, all suave and sexy with that corporate alpha male sex appeal. Love and lust were two different things, and she'd confused the two badly.

It's just seven hours. He probably won't even talk to you. He'll be glued to his phone or laptop, and you will be too.

She halted next to his seat as she shoved her purse into the overhead bin and then looked expectantly at him. He didn't look up. Just like she thought. *Arrogant asshole.*

"Hi, I'm so sorry, but I have the window seat. We can switch if you want..."

He lifted his dark gold brows and his light hazel eyes flicked up to hers. With an exaggerated sigh, he rose from his seat and stepped into the aisle, allowing her to squeeze by him to the window seat. She shoved her backpack under the seat in front of her and settled into the cushy first-class seat.

Oh yeah, first class was definitely amazing. She was going to owe the countess one heck of a Christmas present for this plane ticket.

Her not-so-charming seatmate removed his jacket and folded it, stowing it in the overhead compartment. He was facing her, but his face wasn't visible because of the overhead bin. He rolled up the sleeves of his pale blue dress shirt. Even though their seats weren't squished together like they would be in coach, she could smell a soft blend of pine and spice with a natural masculine aroma. Damn, so Mr. Gorgeous smelled amazing. Well, at least that was a plus and not a minus. Brie focused on the window, watching the ground crews loading bags as she heard the man settle back into his seat.

While the rest of the passengers boarded, she retrieved a book from her backpack to distract herself. She preferred her e-reader when she traveled, but she'd misplaced her charger the day before and her poor e-reader was sitting dead on her nightstand back in her apartment in Chicago.

Luckily, she had a stack of books on her to-be-read pile. This one was a pirate themed historical romance. The bodice ripper cover was a tad embarrassing, even though she secretly liked those covers, and she adored the author. She carefully angled the book's cover toward the window.

When she was fairly certain she wouldn't attract any attention, she peeped at her sexy seatmate. He had his laptop out and was reviewing spreadsheets. The way he was staring—no, *glaring*—at the screen, along with the scowl and stubborn set of his chin, meant he wasn't happy with what he was seeing.

Brie wondered what he did for a living. Something

fancy, or intense. He wore an expensive tailored suit and even the rough, yet artfully-styled look of his hair screamed money. Was it the alpha vibes he was putting out that was attracting her? How did men do that? Just sit there and ooze sexuality?

He noticed her watching him, turned slowly to look at her and raised a brow. God, the man could do so much with his eyebrows. She felt like she'd just been caught watching him undress or something.

"Sorry," she muttered and focused on her book again. This time she did manage to get lost in the story, at least until the plane started rolling down the runway. At that point, she abandoned her book and gripped the armrests in a white knuckle hold and closed her eyes. This was happening. This was really happening. Hours and hours of flying way too damn high over nothing but ocean.

"Are you all right?" A deep British accent asked. She opened one eye to see her seatmate watching her. That voice had been exactly what she would have expected from him: deep and sexy as hell.

"Er...nope," she whispered. "I just hate flying. Like any sane person." She spoke in short bursts, too afraid to keep talking about her fear. It would only make it worse.

"You're going to be fine. Just don't think about it,"

the man replied. His British accent was going a long way to distract her. He could read a grocery list and it would sound amazing.

"Can you keep talking, please?" she asked, closing her eyes again as the plane began to rumble faster down the runway.

"You want me to talk to you?" He sounded half-amused and half-annoyed by her request.

"I'm sorry, it's just...your voice is nice and distracting."

The man chuckled. "You know, most people would just pop an Ambien or Benadryl and it's lights out." He snapped his fingers.

"Most people might, but I'm not about to do that. Fall asleep on an airplane headed to a foreign country? No chance. My cousin works as a paralegal for a law firm that defends airlines. You wouldn't believe what she tells me happens to some female passengers."

"Color me intrigued," the man said.

Brie was about to speak but the plane chose that moment to power up and her body was flattened back against her seat as it gained momentum. She tried not to look out the window to see how fast the runway was zipping by. In fact, she shut her eyes as tight as she gripped her seat, which was pretty damn tight.

After a minute or so, the rumble lessened, and the sense of acceleration dropped.

"We're in the air," the man said more quietly, his tone gentle. She opened her eyes to see him leaning back in his chair, watching her with an unreadable expression.

The plane now shifted in the air, dipping down enough to send her stomach roiling as she recognized a few seconds of them freefalling. The horizon dipped out her window. They were making a turn.

"I really hate this. We're stuck in a huge metal deathtrap."

"Let me guess." He steepled his fingers as he continued to look at her. "You don't travel."

"Oh, I travel," she shot back, her temper flaring. She didn't like that he was implying she was a coward. "I just hate planes."

He made a low noise in the back of his throat that sounded disbelieving. She wanted to argue with him, but he leaned over and pulled the romance novel out of her lap and flipped it over to see the cover. He burst out laughing the second he saw it.

"Do you *mind?*" She pried one of her hands off the armrest to grab the book, but he swatted her hand away.

"This trash entertains you?"

"*Trash*? It's not trash, you..." She bit her lip to keep from calling him an asshole. She usually had much better control of herself, but something about this guy set her on edge. Gorgeous men always did.

"Come now. All of it is bodice ripping mommy por—"

"Don't say it!" She made another attempt to get her book back, but he leaned far enough away that she missed and her hand smacked his stomach. He had a hard, muscled abdomen, because of course he did. The man now thumbed through a random section of the book.

"Let's see here... Heaving bosoms, a pirate lord, an arrogant naval officer who wants to marry the heroine. Yes, this is most definitely—"

Before he could finish, Brie unclipped her seatbelt and lunged at him, half landing on his lap as she struggled to free her book from his hands. He released the book immediately to grip her hips and steady her. If he hadn't, she would have taken a swan dive into the first-class aisle with economy-class grace.

"Very well, take your book back Miss..."

"Honeyweather, Brie Honeyweather."

"Brie?"

"Brie. B-R-I-E."

"Like the cheese?" He laughed, drawing the attention of the man across the aisle. She became keenly aware that she was still sitting on the British asshole's lap while she should have been strapped down by the window. Brie pulled free of him and sat back in her own seat, clutching her book.

"It's short for Breanna."

The asshole was still laughing at her.

"What's your name? Or should I just call you Mr. Asshat?"

"You may call me whatever you like, *Brie*." He emphasized her name with another chuckle. "Or you can call me Alec."

Alec. Of course, he had a sexy sort of name. It couldn't have been something silly like Eugene or Percy, something that would have lessened that British sex appeal.

"Well, Alec, I wish I could say it's nice to meet you but...well..." She trailed off, feeling a tinge of guilt at her catty remark. It wasn't like her at all.

She was not usually this rude, but this guy made it impossible to be nice. Maybe it was because he reminded her of Preston, and she was determined to see every flaw in advance. Not that she's stood a chance of a guy like this. Not that she wanted to.

She was twenty-nine with a job that she could do from home, and she'd embraced her single life quite comfortably. She'd bet anything that this guy always dated models. Brie knew she was attractive, but she wasn't a model; she was too curvy to pull off that waifish look, and she was only five foot five.

She tried to focus on her book, but soon gave up. After she retrieved her laptop from her bag, she pulled up her notes for the countess's Christmas book and started plotting out chapters based on some of the events events that the countess said took place at Merryvale Court during the holidays. From the corner of her eye, she noticed that Alex opened his own laptop back up. Both were lost in their own work for at least an hour.

By the time the flight attendants came by to serve drinks and dinner, she was starving.

"Filet mignon or chicken Parmesan?" The flight attendant asked Alec with a broad smile. The young woman practically leaned on the seat in front of him, displaying her figure to her best advantage to catch his attention.

Alec's eyes swept over her, but it wasn't a very interested look, at least from what Brie could tell.

"The filet, please. Thank you."

The attendant turned to her. "And you, miss?"

"The same."

"For drinks we have this menu." The attendant

passed them a copy of the menu and Alec politely leaned left to let Brie see it at the same time.

"A Diet Coke," Brie said.

"You're in first class and you order a Diet Coke?" Alec muttered in disgust. Then he turned to the attendant. "A bottle of champagne, please. Two glasses."

"Yes sir," the attendant smiled once more at Alec, the invitation quite clear, but Alec only smiled back politely at the woman.

"You'll try the champagne," he informed Brie.

"Not very likely. You don't seem like someone I'd want to share a drink with."

"Because I took your book?"

"And made fun of it. Oh yes, I'd *love* to share a glass of champagne with you. You probably only read Salman Rushdie or Pulitzer Prize nominees, or *Proust*." She then put her finger to the tip of her nose and pushed it up as high as it would go.

"Charming behavior."

"Hey, you started it. Don't dish it out if you can't take it."

"Very well. I was simply trying to do you a favor."

"A *favor*?"

"If you don't enjoy first-class, you aren't doing the thing properly, are you?" When he said this, it sounded so perfectly British, like she was sitting next to a modern day Mr. Darcy.

"Okay fine. Twist my arm. It's not like I'm buying." This time when he smiled, he turned the full wattage on her. He hadn't done *that* with the attendant. The expression knocked the breath from her. Damn, he had a gorgeous smile. It was slightly mischievous, as though whatever caused the smile was going to be trouble. *He* was trouble and she was stuck with him for the next seven hours.

2

lec Halston had expected a nice quiet flight to London. After two intense weeks overseeing the setup of a new investment banking division at Barclays in Chicago, he was glad to be heading home. The work had been exciting, but now he was exhausted and on the edge of burnout. Knowing he had more work waiting for him back in London only added to his sense of fatigue. This flight was his only chance to rest before getting back into the chaos at his office, and he'd expected to sleep most of the flight.

What he hadn't expected was this puzzling contradiction of a woman sitting beside him. She seemed to be close to his own age, maybe a little younger. She had that mix of intellect and innocence he didn't often see in his social circles. With her battered romance novel and delightfully witty reactions to his biting humor, he felt more energized by the minute.

This woman was different...and that was surprisingly refreshing. She was attractive too, which didn't help his plan to not get involved with anyone. He just couldn't help himself; he enjoyed pushing her buttons. There was something delightful about the hint of a smile she had when she talked, even when she was clearly frustrated with him. It made a man wonder how it would feel to kiss those lips into silence in the middle of an argument and see them soften into a broad smile as she looked up at him.

The fall of her dark brown hair was straight and shiny, almost like silk. Most women he'd known used products that made the strands crinkle when he tried to run his hands through them. With Brie, he could tell just by looking how soft her hair would be. It was too bad he had no excuse to reach over and verify. Then again, she'd literally fallen onto his lap earlier and damn if that hadn't been almost as good. He knew he was an arse for thinking that, but he did enjoy it.

Normally these flights were long and boring, but now things were getting interesting. His initial frustration at having this Brie Honeyweather share his row had faded. He was rather entertained with disrupting her. He liked the way her cheeks colored and her eyes widened when he had surprised her with his inappropriate behavior.

The flight attendant returned with a bottle and glasses. "Your champagne." The bottle was already opened, and she poured two glasses and set them on the attached tray Alec had flipped down. He handed Brie her glass.

"Er... I really don't think I need—"

"Take it. Just don't drink too fast. The alcohol has a greater effect at this altitude." Alec took a sip. It wasn't bad...for airline champagne.

"Thank you," Brie blushed again, and he resisted the urge to grin. Yes, spending the next few hours toying with her would be quite entertaining.

She sipped her champagne and her eyes lit up in delight.

"A champagne fan?" he asked. "I thought all you Americans preferred beer."

She narrowed her eyes. "I'm not into beer. Wine is okay, but I *love* champagne," she admitted with another blush. The tension in her body relaxed and she eased into her seat.

"So, what brings you to London, Ms. Honeyweather."

"Brie," she corrected.

"Brie. Lord, I'm sorry," he laughed. "I just keep

thinking I should eat you with some crackers...or perhaps some grapes."

The second his innuendo registered, her face turned red. "Just when I thought you were starting to be nice."

"I'm teasing. Please, do tell me what brings you to London."

"I'm a ghostwriter." She nudged the edge of her backpack under the seat with a toe of her brown boot.

"A ghostwriter? What do you write?"

"Mostly nonfiction. I work with people who have lived amazing lives, gone on incredible journeys, or made incredible discoveries. But they don't always have natural writing talent. When they work with me, I bring magic and structure to their stories."

"It sounds like you enjoy your job," he mused as he twisted his champagne glass by the stem.

"I do." She looked up at him, her confidence return-ing. "What do you do? Oh wait, I bet I can guess." She twisted in her seat to eye him critically and tilted her head slightly as she held her drink.

"Oh? And what am I then?" He set his glass down on his tray and crossed his arms, offering her his most charming smile, the one that made even married women consider hiding their wedding rings.

"You are..." She squinted one eye, and the adorable

expression on her face almost made him laugh. "An investment banker."

"Bravo!" He leaned toward her a little, closing the distance between them. "What gave me away?"

She rested her chin on her hand as they stared at each other, only a few inches apart. A spark traveled between them and damned if he wasn't tempted to close the distance and kiss this stranger. He'd had sex a few times on a plane but that was only for fun when there was a thrill. And for some reason this woman, the opposite of his usual tastes, was thrilling the hell out of him. He usually dated tall leggy blondes who looked like they came right off the runway, and she was the opposite of all that.

He was completely fascinated with Brie's soft, natural appearance and the playful relaxed way she interacted with him. There was a hint of sexual interest from her; he could see it every time her blue eyes swept down his body, but she wasn't trying to lure him in or catch him. If anything, he sensed she was fighting to keep her distance.

"What gave you away?" she repeated softly, drawing out her explanation in a way that tantalized him. He had to admit he liked her voice. It wasn't husky and low, nor was it high and girlish. It had hints of energetic delight, yet it was tempered by a soft sensual note. Forget writing books, the woman should narrate them.

"Yes, tell me, what revealed my job?"

"Expensive leather briefcase…" She squinted one eye again as though peering through a microscope. "Your perfectly tailored suit, that haircut—"

He reached up to drag his hands through his hair. "What's wrong with my hair?" he demanded.

She giggled, the effects of the champagne were starting to show. "Nothing," she replied with wide, guileless eyes that didn't fool him one bit.

"Then what did you mean?"

She gestured vaguely at his head. "You know."

"No, darling. I don't have the faintest idea what you're talking about." He rather liked his hair. To think that it might be… what was he thinking? His hair was just *fine*.

"It has that whole overly perfect look to it," she explained and took another drink of her champagne, emptying the flute.

"It's *not* overly styled." He took his time each morning to get the look just right. It wasn't overdone. He was certain of that.

"It *so* is," Brie asserted confidently. "You need it more like—" She leaned over, closing the distance between them and dug her hands into his hair. It was clear she was messing up his hair.

"Very funny," he grumbled.

"I thought so." She winked at him, but her hands didn't leave his hair.

Fuck... Her fingers threading through his hair felt good. Too good. He tried to prevent himself from being aroused by her touch, but it wasn't easy. She ran her fingers through his hair a few more seconds, biting her lip in a way that did not help his condition whatsoever. Maybe he should just get her into the bathroom and—

"Like that." She pulled her hands free of his hair, but he reached out and caught her wrists before she could retreat.

"I'm almost afraid to go look," he muttered. His hair was probably standing completely on end. Alec brushed his thumbs against the skin of her wrists before letting go.

She laughed. "You *have* to go look, don't you?"

"Yes, I'm afraid so." He slid off the seat and went to the first-class bathroom and peered at himself in the mirror. His hair wasn't mussed up. It was...good. It was perfectly touched up the way he liked, though it did look a little like he'd just made love to a woman and she'd been running her fingers through it. The thought gave him too many tempting ideas about Brie. He placed his hands on the counter and closed his eyes.

Think of primary school, or algebra... Anything other than what it would be like to pin Brie up against the counter and pull down those jeans she's wearing and—

"Bloody Christ." He drew in a dozen breaths before he regained enough control to leave the bathroom.

When Alec returned to his seat, he found dinner waiting on his tray table. Brie had poured herself another glass of champagne and was swiping through the in-flight movie selections.

Alec sat down and unrolled the silverware from his cloth napkin. "Anything good?"

"Some rom-coms, a few thrillers, and a couple of documentaries." Brie mused as she continued to swipe through the available shows.

"You'd better eat before it gets cold." He pushed her tray toward her.

Brie glanced his way and smiled. "You didn't fix your hair."

"I thought you did a fine job and didn't want to waste your efforts," he lied. The truth was he couldn't stay in that bathroom without indulging in a fantasy that would lead to trouble. Trouble was the last thing he needed. Even though he enjoyed a quick hookup, he did not want to do that on a seven-hour flight, no matter how cute Brie was or how her mouth was making it very hard for him to think straight.

"So, you're a native Londoner?" she asked as she cut into her filet.

"Not really. I grew up in the country outside of Manchester before attending Eton and Cambridge."

"I have a question about that. Why do Cambridge and Oxford have all these colleges within the main university?" She took a bite of her filet and made a sweet little sound of pleasure. "What's up with that?"

"Ah. No, I see your confusion. It's not like they are separate schools," he paused, thinking over how best to explain it. "It is more like residence halls that you would have at a University. So, if a student stays at King's College, that would be the location of his or her room, perhaps even their dining hall for lunch and dinner. Some colleges were established with religious purposes hundreds of years ago, though the religious connections may no longer exist."

"Okay..." She paused, seeming to think it over. "So what college were you?"

"The King's College of Our Lady and St. Nicholas in Cambridge." He could see he had her full attention. This woman liked history and he could bloody well deliver on that. "It was founded in 1441, but its construction was disrupted by the War of the Roses. It was finally finished in 1544 and has the world's largest fan vaulted ceiling in its chapel. Notable alumni include Robert Walpole, the first prime minister of England, and E.M. Forster, the novelist." He recited what he remembered from his first tour of the college all those years ago.

Brie's eyes lit with a fervent light as she began to recite a passage from one of Forster's books. "*I used to be so dreamy about a man's love as a girl, and think that, for good or evil, love must be the great thing. But it hasn't been, it has been itself a dream.*"

"*Howard's End?*" Alec confirmed and she nodded. "Well said. That was the only book I read of his, but it was excellent."

Howard's End was the story of a strong-willed, intelligent woman who refused to let her husband and his family ruin her life with their smugness and pride. It was not a romance, not like her bodice ripping pirate story.

She seemed to realize the direction of his thoughts. "I don't just read romance," she replied. "But I enjoy stories with happy endings the best."

"Why? Real life rarely ends happily. At best, it ends in a draw." His tone came out a little more belligerent than he'd intended.

"Perhaps that's why. People need to *believe* in

things. Love, heroes, adventures, a purpose to a life that might otherwise feel purposeless. Romance gives people hope." She grinned. "And the books are just fun. What do you read? And please, for the love of God, tell me you read and not something predictable like *Hemingway*. So many people don't read anymore." The way she said that, with a note of subtle sorrow intrigued him. Someone who had mattered to her most must not have been a reader.

"I read," he assured her. "Mostly nonfiction. True crime tends to be my favorite, but I admit I have a soft spot for Agatha Christie mysteries. I blame my mother for it."

"*Murder on the Orient Express*?" Brie asked.

"*Death on the Nile* is my favorite. But *Orient* is very good. *And Then There Were None* is also a classic. Even though I know how they all end, I always like to reread them. There's something to the way she weaves all the characters together until you're left questioning whether you really do remember how it ends or who the murderer actually was."

"I think I watched more Hercule Poirot movies than I've read the books," Brie admitted with a blush. "David Suchet was such a perfect choice for him."

"I agree. My mom loves the old Poirot show. I've caught her watching reruns more than once." He couldn't help but grin. It had been ages since he'd thought of how his mum would put a kettle on and settle in her favorite parlor to watch Poirot. He rarely went home anymore... and he especially avoided that place on Christmas. It was too painful. Even now the thought made his chest tight as he closed his eyes a second too long.

Brie's warm fingertips touched his hand, drawing him back to the plane. "Are you okay?"

"Yes. Sorry. Just thinking." He tried to return to the subject. "I must admit I have a certain fondness for Kenneth Branagh's recent take on the detective. Sometimes a new interpretation brings fresh energy to a well-known story."

They finished dinner and the attendants cleared their plates. They were given a small leather tote containing lip balm, toothpaste, a hairbrush, hand sanitizer, and lotion. When the cabin lights dimmed, many of the passengers around them pressed the button to flatten their seats into beds for the night.

"A real bed," Brie sighed dreamily. "The last time I flew overnight was when I was in college. I flew in coach and I can't sleep sitting up."

"Nor can I," Alec agreed. It was why he'd made Barclays pay for first class. He couldn't sleep with all those people crammed in around him.

"Do you mind if I...?" She held up her toiletry kit and nodded at the bathroom.

"Sure." He stood to let her pass, straightening as she brushed against him. He was lost for a moment in the feel of her body pressed to his. Then his stomach dropped as the plane tilted. He reacted instinctively, grasping Brie's hips. She clutched his chest to keep from toppling into the row across from them. His hands tightened and he fought hard not to do something completely reckless like steal a kiss in the middle of a crowded plane.

"Thanks," she murmured, and he reluctantly let go. Something was wrong with him. He'd become fixated on this woman. He needed to focus on work. He waited for Brie to return and then used the bathroom after her, brushing his teeth and using the facilities. When he got back to their row, she was trying to fix her bed without success.

"Alec, I'm sorry to bug you but—"

"I'll see to it." He leaned past her to turn her seat into a bed and then handed her the pillow and blanket that came with her seat. It was only when he'd settled into his own bed that he realized just how close he was to Brie. Lying down in the dark, their breath mingled as they faced one another.

"You know, for a *smart Alec*, you really aren't so bad," she whispered.

The dimmed cabin lights reflected as tiny pinpricks of light in her eyes, like distant stars in a cold winter sky. There was no denying that she was lovely. The inviting shape of her mouth, the heart-shaped face, and the impish curve of her nose, all now shadowed, were no less attractive than before. But the quiet and the dark lent a fresh intimacy between them that sent a forbidden thrill through him.

"You aren't too bad either, *Cheddar*," he said.

"Cheddar?"

"What?" he smirked. "It's better than Brie."

"Oh my god, I kind of hate you." But she was laughing as she said it and there was a delightful twinkle in her eyes that he enjoyed.

Brie's smile was soft and sleepy. She fisted a hand against her mouth when she yawned. "Thanks for keeping me distracted during takeoff...and for the champagne."

"You're welcome," he answered and watched her close her eyes. The sight of her falling asleep was strangely fascinating. As a child, he'd teased his cousin, Astrid, for loving the movie *Sleeping Beauty*. He laughed at the idea of a man being bewitched by a sleeping woman he didn't know, but now he knew what the prince had felt in that moment in the film. There was a magnetic need to be close to this woman. He craved to know what dreams might come into her mind, what adventures she would encounter in the place between deep sleep and waking.

What is it about you, Brie Honeyweather, that makes me forget... That makes me hunger... And the longer he looked at her, he did hunger for so many things. The strongest of which was for a kiss he would never have.

BRIE'S BED SHOOK SLIGHTLY, THE TURBULENCE WAKING HER. She rolled on her back and groaned as she realized where she was. On a plane. Somewhere over the Atlantic Ocean. Hurtling through the atmosphere at hundreds of miles an hour.

"You okay?" Alec's voice was roughened with sleep. It startled her for a moment. Their drowsy gazes locked, and she couldn't deny the quiet intimacy of the moment, as though they were the only two people there. The plane was so quiet it was easy to believe that narrative.

"Yeah, I'm okay." She then realized with some embarrassment that she needed to go to the bathroom.

"I'm sorry, but I'm going up to crawl over you to use the restroom."

He stayed still as she did exactly that. Once inside, she looked at herself in the mirror and wondered how much sleep she actually got. She'd put her watch in her backpack before she got to security and forgotten to put it back on. She washed her hands and opened the door but gasped when she saw Alec standing just outside.

"Alec, what are you—?"

He stepped into the restroom with her and closed the door, locking it shut.

"Shh…" He held a finger to his lips and flashed her a smile that woke every last bit of her feminine side up. He was all man in that moment as he cornered her against the sink and cupped her face, kissing her hard.

"Alec…what are we doing?" She gasped against his mouth.

"We are enjoying ourselves," he said. "Unless you don't want this?" He kissed the path from her mouth down her neck, pulling at the soft cream-colored sweater she'd worn to bed.

"I…" Oh hell, she did want this. It had been so damn long. She pulled at the buttons of his suit shirt which was crumpled from sleep. "*Yes.*"

"Thank God," he growled. He tugged his shirt open so she could run her palms over his chest, feeling his glorious muscled abdomen. Just like she'd hoped for. He was perfect, he was here, and he was hers, even if for just a few minutes.

He brushed a palm over her breast above her bra, thumbing her nipple through the fabric which hardened to peak between his hand and the lacy cloth. "How do you want it?"

"Um, not sure." She gasped as he suddenly spun her to face the mirror and pressed her against the counter from behind.

"This okay?" he asked as he nipped her earlobe. An almost violent zinging pleasure shot straight to her womb and she hissed.

"Yes...like that... Oh *fuck*." She moaned as he slid a hand under the front of her jeans to cup her mound.

"You have to be quiet..." He warned in a deliciously dirty voice.

She nodded as he thumbed her clit and she pushed back against him, feeling his shaft pressing against her ass.

"Do it," she begged.

She didn't need to ask a second time. He pulled her jeans down to her thighs and unfastened his own. Then he was thrusting into her, taking her hard, filling her up and fucking her raw. It was the single most glorious moment of her life. She was almost there, climbing the peak toward orgasm as he thrust into her. Almost there. Almost...

Brie shifted, twisting under the thin blanket, confused and aroused as hell in her tiny airplane bed.

Shit. It was a *dream.* Alec was lying next to her in his own pod, sleeping softly, his hair mussed from his pillow. She was tempted to reach out and touch him but didn't dare.

Did I really just dream about him fucking me in the airplane bathroom?

She laid back, resting a hand over her eyes as she felt the flush of heat subside. She really did have to go to the bathroom, though. She sat up, pushed the blanket aside, and faced the sleeping form of Alec currently in her way.

She carefully stretched her leg over his body and planted it on the ground in the aisle but with a sudden movement of his knee beneath her, she fell on top of him.

"*Oof!*" He grunted, followed quickly by, "*Fuck!*" as he woke up. "What the—?" He stared up at her with a confused half-asleep expression.

"Sorry," she whispered. The last thing she wanted to do was wake everyone else up in first class.

"What the bloody hell are you doing?" He growled in that sleep roughened voice, exactly like in her dream.

"I need to use the restroom," she said.

"Did you have to knee me in the bullocks?" he muttered.

"I'm sorry," she said again, "You shifted. I lost my balance." Her face heated as she struggled to get off him.

"Hold still." He put his hands on her ass as he tried to reposition her so she could slide off him and into the aisle.

"I really am sorry," she said, getting her balance back.

"Just go." He waved a hand at her and she rushed to the bathroom. She stared at her tired, puffy eyes in the mirror and her embarrassed reddened cheeks. What if he followed her to the bathroom? What if she opened the door and he'd be standing there, ready to...?

That was ridiculous. She opened the door and faced the empty aisle. But more than a small part of her had hoped he would be standing there like in her dream. She buried the twinge of disappointment as she returned to her seat. When she got back to their row, he was still awake.

"Up and over you go," he said as she stepped over him and lay back down on her own bed. "Watch the knees."

"Did I really hurt you?"

He sighed, the sound deep and aggrieved. "No. A man doesn't need his balls."

"I didn't do it on purpose."

"Brie?" he whispered in a voice that was almost silky now.

Her heart skipped a few beats as remnants of her dream came back. "What?"

"Go to sleep." She huffed and then froze as he spoke again. "And stop moaning. It's driving me mad."

"Moan? I wasn't—"

"Oh, you were," he insisted. "Whatever you were dreaming was either terrible or excellent. Either way, it was keeping me awake."

"Asshole," she muttered.

"I heard that," he growled. And for some reason she found herself smiling as she closed her eyes.

Breakfast in first class was decent, with omelets, French toast, and coffee from a press. None of that powdery day-old charcoal-tasting stuff the main cabin would be served.

Alec ate as he scanned *Wall Street Journal* headlines on his phone. Brie had her laptop out and was typing while she nibbled at her French toast. He peeked once or twice at her screen and saw some kind of timeline for a book about English Christmas traditions. He winced and turned away. The last thing he wanted to think about were traditions, the past, and least of all Christmas. He turned back to his phone, answering a few quick emails about when he would be back in the office. Even though he would be returning to the airport later this evening, he could at least work half the day.

He gave Brie another glance as the flight attendant collected their breakfast trays.

"You never told me how you ended up flying first class," he said. It was her first time in first class and the idea had been tugging at him. "Most people don't fly this way unless they have a good reason." He suspected being a ghost writer didn't pay a lot, at least not enough to fly first class.

"My client paid for it, actually. She insisted. I told her I didn't need to, but she was set on me not having an uncomfortable trip over here."

"I see. And you writing a book for her about…?" He trailed off, expecting her to answer.

"I can't really discuss this project. I signed a nondisclosure agreement about the identity of the client and the nature of the project."

That piqued his interest. "Is she a political figure? Wait, you aren't interviewing the Prime Minister or the Queen are you?" he teased.

She laughed, relaxing a little. "No one that famous. But the client is still a bit of a rock star to me, I guess."

"So, a musician?" He set his phone down. "Adele? Lily Allen? Madonna's back in London, I hear…"

"Stop guessing. Seriously, I can't tell you." She was still laughing but she glanced down at his lap. "I am sorry about last night, by the way. I didn't mean to knee you in the...you know."

Alec shrugged, trying to forget the memory of that honey sweet smell of her that invaded his senses even as his body had bucked in pain at the collision. For the rest of the night, with her soft moans a foot away from him, he'd been half hard just from the drowsy sound of her voice.

"It's fine. I shall persevere." He lifted his chin nobly and she half laughed, covering her reddening face with her hands. He reached over and gently pried her palms away so he could look at her.

"I'm only kidding."

She changed the subject. "So, you're headed home?"

"Yes. Time enough for a shower and then back to work. You?"

"I'm catching another flight from here later today to an airport near to my client."

"They're not in London?"

"No." But she didn't reveal anything more. She turned back to her work and he to his.

Once the plane started to descend, he remembered her fear of flying. He looked at her and saw her white knuckled grip on the arm rests. He reached over and put a hand over hers without a word and she relaxed ever so slightly. The plane hit the runway and the bounced a second or two before the squeal of tires signaled they were slowing down.

"Thanks," she said as she as the plane slowed and started taxiing to the gate.

"My pleasure."

As the plane stopped and the seatbelt sign clicked off, the people around them all stood. He opened the bin above him, grabbed her purse, and handed it to her.

"Thanks." She took it and slung her backpack on. Alec was tempted to ask for her number, but he stopped. He didn't have time for a fling and neither did she. She was off to parts unknown and he had to head to work.

"It was nice to meet you," she said, and their hands briefly met in a polite shake. It seemed so...unsatisfying.

"Safe travels," he said as he let her leave ahead of him. And just like that, she was gone. He retrieved his jacket from the overhead bin and then pulled the handle on his rolling briefcase to start down the aisle.

"Sir!" An attendant called after him. She held up the battered romance novel.

"That's not mine" But it was no use. Brie would be long gone. He accepted the book and tucked it into his briefcase.

Once off the plane, he checked the crowds milling by the gate but didn't see her. And he had no way to contact her about her book. He could try looking her up on social media later... As silly as that sounded it was his only option.

He caught a black cab back to his flat at Regent's Crescent. Alec stepped out of the cab and rolled his suitcase up the steps into the magnificent two-story lobby. It was bathed in natural light with sweeping views of the private gardens behind the building.

An imperial split staircase curved down from the entrance to the concierge desk. It was a modern take on the old flats that had been here since the Regency period. Brie would have been interested in that. She would have—

Alec stopped the thought before it could travel any further.

His flat had large windows and lofty ceilings that welcomed in the sun. The surrounding gardens had a host of tall trees which cast shades of green into his rooms in the spring and summer, and golden amber hues in the fall. Even though the white painted walls were modern in style and his furniture clearly set a modern mood, the marble mantle and tall mirrors along with the fireplace and woodworking lent an air of bygone craftsmanship that was rarely seen in the world anymore. There were no family photos, no hints of his past. He preferred it that way.

Look only to the present and the future. That was what his first boss at Barclays had said to him. Alec had let it become a sort of mantra for him.

His mobile vibrated as he set his suitcase and briefcase in his bedroom. He pulled the phone out of his trousers and answered without checking who it was. He assumed it was his assistant, who already knew he would be headed into the office soon.

"Hello?"

"Alec, dear, are you still coming home tonight?" His mother's voice filled him with a sudden pang of longing.

"Yes, mum. I only just got home and was going to shower and head to work for a bit."

"But you worked all last week in Chicago. Your father and I haven't seen you in five months☐"

"Mum," he interrupted gently. "I'll be there tonight, all right?"

"Good," she relaxed. "Thad and his wife arrived today. Their daughter Lyra is such an adorable girl. You will like her. Maybe Thad can convince you it's time to settle down. He did."

"Mum," he warned.

"Don't you *Mum* me." She shot back. "Between you working so much and Morgan... Lord save me from Morgan."

"What's he done now?" Alec asked. His little brother was two years younger than him, at twenty-eight, and he was a notorious flirt.

"I've never seen him with the same girl twice. If neither of you settle down, there will be no one to carry on the name, or the bloody title. It's beginning to stress your father out."

Alec rolled his eyes. His father, Byron Halston, the Earl of Merryvale wasn't worried, at least not yet. When he was, he would be sure to let Alec know. His father was more relaxed than his mother about a lot of things.

Alec winced as his mother nearly shouted. "Morgan! Come talk to your brother. And be sure to tell him how disappointed I am that neither of you are married yet."

He heard some scuffling noises, and then, "Hey *bruv*." Morgan greeted him with a fake Cockney accent straight out of *Eastenders*.

"Stop that. You'll give mum fits," Alec ordered.

Morgan laughed but dropped the accent. "You'd better make it tonight. Mum is losing her mind. She's got all these guests coming and everything has to be perfect, you know?"

Alec knew exactly what Morgan was talking about.

Christmas was his mother's favorite holiday. "Understood. See you tonight, Morgan."

He hung up and tossed the phone on the bed before heading to his bathroom and stripping out of his clothes. When he caught sight of his hair in the mirror, he suddenly chuckled at the mess. No doubt Brie would have approved. As he removed his shirt he stopped and brought the fabric up to his nose. A hint of Brie's scent was still lingered.

He closed his eyes and inhaled deeply as he pictured her face. The blue eyes, the sensual lips, her hair sweeping down to form a rich waterfall as she fell on top of him.

His body responded at the memory and he tried to ignore the blood flowing straight to his cock, but it was hard not to think of her. He ditched his remaining clothes and got into the white marble shower stall. His body was rigid beneath the hot spray as he took himself in hand and stroked until he found release.

Gasping softly, he leaned back against the heated marble and blew out a breath. He wondered if she would ever think of him again. Would she be haunted by their one night together? A night charged with subtle tensions, like a building storm? He knew he would...

WHEN ALEC REACHED HIS OFFICE, HIS MOBILE WAS BLOWING up with work calls and emails. He threw himself into his chair and spun to face the skyrise view of London's financial district, prepared to answer the endless emails and voice messages on his phone. Christ, he had so much to do.

The Chicago assignment had been exciting, but he was glad to be home. Of course, that meant catching up on everything he missed while he was gone. Seven days was the equivalent of half a year's work for an investment banker. He worked impossibly long hours and saw more of the showers in his office building than at his own home.

Alec turned back to his desk and knocked his briefcase over. The pirate romance novel slid across the wood floor. He scrambled to pick it up before someone noticed, but it was too late.

"A bit of light reading?" Nathan Montgomery asked from the doorway. The other man's eyes settled on the book on the floor between them, his lip curling in a mocking sneer.

"Stow it, Monty," he snapped. Nathan was the office piranha. Whenever he smelled blood in the water, he started feeding with a frenzy. He was not anyone's friend.

Nathan changed tact. "How was Chicago? You missed a lot here last week."

Alec raised a brow. Nathan was a scrappy fellow who'd worked his way up in the world. Alec would have admired him under normal circumstances, but Nathan had been raised in the East End in a slum and held a grudge against just about everyone, especially someone like Alec. Nathan saw him as nothing more than a spoiled brat born with a silver spoon in his mouth. The future Earl of Merryvale. Alec represented everything Nathan despised. And it pissed Alec off.

"If you don't have something relevant to say..." he warned.

Nathan's wiry frame tensed as he sensed he'd pushed too far. "Mr. Eppley wants to see you." Nathan's mouth twisted into a smirk as he walked off.

Fucking nutter. Always trying to stir things up. Alec tucked the pirate romance back into his attaché case and headed down to his boss's office.

Howard Eppley was an old lion compared to the young bloods that filled most of the offices on their floor. Investment banking demanded energy and excitement, and most men burned out by the time they were forty. Eppley hadn't. He'd made the transition to vice president and now supervised men like Alec, which left him well above the demands of time and energy that broke the backs of the younger men beneath him.

Alec rapped his knuckles on the half open door. "Mr. Eppley?"

"That you, Halston?" Eppley called out. "Come in."

Alex looked inside the corner office. Eppley held a putter and was lining up to hit a ball into a sleek black coffee mug on the floor. At fifty-four, Eppley was still fit, even though his dark hair was streaked with gray at the temples. He was on wife number three, surprisingly not for infidelity but simply because the first two had not understood the nature of the job or its demands. He was still good friends with both of them.

"Glad to see you survived Chicago. Those chaps in America make us look like we're on a bloody holiday all the time." Eppley lined up a shot and putted. The ball rolled twelve feet over an expensive oriental carpet and bounced into and back out of the cup. Eppley grinned and set his putter aside before looking seriously at Alec.

"Word hasn't gotten around the office yet, but we'll be handling a huge merger over Christmas and through the New Year. I would like for you to be in charge. Monty knows something is up, but I don't like him. He'd sell his own gran if it made him look good." Eppley leaned against his desk. "Can I count on you to handle it?"

"Absolutely, sir. I will be in the country for the holidays, but I assume I'll be able to handle things remotely."

"I thought you didn't care for the holidays?"

Alec shrugged. "I don't, but the family is insisting this year."

"Yes, of course. Well, If you're sure you can handle it when the paperwork comes in."

"I can, sir."

As Alec turned to leave, Eppley spoke again. "Be careful, Halston. You'll be facing some big decisions soon and the paths offered will be very different."

Alec slid his hands into his trouser pockets and gazed at the skyline of Eppley's window. He knew what his boss was hinting at.

"Which path did you choose?"

Eppley was quiet a moment. "Looking back? Not the right one. People in this line of work are either desperate to prove something or desperate to escape something. Make sure you're here for the right reasons."

Alec could only nod before he left Eppley's office. Did he want to prove something or was he running from something? His mouth suddenly tasted bitter as he realized it just might be a bit of both.

BURNING TWELVE HOURS IN THE AIRPORT WAS NOT EASY, especially when Brie realized she'd lost her book. She'd returned to the gate to check with the crew from her plane, but they were already gone. Then she'd been forced to go through customs, collect her luggage and check in for her next flight. After that she'd gone to the nearest bookshop by her gate and bought a couple of romance novels by her favorite author, the same stories that had been filmed at Merryvale Court. Of course, in the books the house was called something else. She'd already read the entire series but couldn't resist the urge to reread them.

She'd also bought some snacks and hopped between gates as her flight to Manchester kept changing gates for some reason. By early evening, she was desperate to get on her plane and get out of the airport. When the attendant at the gate finally started calling first class, she collected her things and headed to the growing line.

"Excuse me." She bumped into a tall man with dark gold hair.

The man stepped aside as she passed. "Sorry."

She froze. "Alec?" She'd spent all day trying to forget him and the feeling of leaving something important undone when she hadn't asked him for his number or email.

He blinked in equal shock. "Brie?"

"Yeah..." She swept her gaze over his body.

He'd lost the suit and wore a black sweater that clung to his broad muscled shoulders and hung a bit looser at his tapered waist. His jeans were snug, but not too snug. He looked...good. Maybe even better than before. Brie knew it was just her libido talking but *damn*...he made her forget every promise she'd ever made to be rational when it came to picking men. It really was like Preston all over again. She totally had a type and that was not a good thing.

"You're on this flight?" she asked.

"I am... You are too?" Alec bent to open his briefcase and pulled out a book. *Her* book. "You left this behind on the last flight."

"God, you found it!" She accepted the book with a grin but couldn't resist teasing him. "Why don't you keep it? I own the audio edition."

"Of course, you do," he replied with a roll of his eyes but he returned the book to his briefcase.

"So...you're headed to Manchester?" She got in line behind him as they started to board.

"Spending the holidays with my family."

She picked on up on his reluctance. "Not looking forward to it?"

"I despise the holidays. They are unpleasant."

Wow, that she hadn't expected. Such a blunt answer...and a sad one at that.

"Is it the holiday or the family that bothers you?"

Alec spoke over his shoulder as he stepped onto the plane ahead of her. "My grandfather died on Christmas Day. I don't really like to talk about it." This time his tone carried a heavy finality that warned her not to probe any deeper.

He paused and glanced down at his ticket. "What seat are you?"

She glanced at her boarding pass. "6A... Window seat."

"6B." He shook his head and with a chuckle stepped back to let her slip past him. He accepted her purse without even asking and put it in the overhead bin above them. As he sat down beside her, she caught a fresh scent of a pine scent mixed with aftershave.

"Ugh, you got to shower, didn't you?" She accused.

He smirked, that bad boy expression turning every

bit of her on. "Yes, I did. All that hot water... It was glorious."

"I hate you," she muttered.

He nudged her arm with his, making a grand show of getting comfortable in his chair. This plane was tiny compared to the first one. Brie's nerves started to build as she looked at the fog that was the beginning to roll through the airport outside.

"You should relax. The flight is only an hour or so."

Brie swallowed hard and went to grip the handle of the armrest, but his hand was in the way. She started to pull away, but he closed his eyes and turned his palm face up, in silent invitation. She hesitated for only a moment before she placed her palm in his. Then he laced their fingers and held her hand tight enough to reassure her.

"Just relax," he murmured again. The plane only seated thirty people and soon the cabin doors were secured and the plane was ready to take off.

It's going to be fine, just fine. The more she mentally echoed this, the more it felt like a lie. The plane taxied out to the runway and then ramped up its speed before lifting into the night. The pilot came on, announcing the weather and foggy conditions.

"You okay?" Alec asked.

She opened her eyes, waiting for the plane to reach

its height before it dipped as she knew it would. "Yeah, the fog makes me nervous."

"They know how to fly in fog. They've done it plenty of times." He glanced toward where the attendant was in her jumpsuit. "Maybe when the drink cart comes, we can order champagne again."

"Good plan." Brie's stomach pitched as the plane dropped a little then steadied out.

"See? All is well." Alec didn't let go of her hand until the attendant unclipped her seatbelt and began serving drinks from the drink cart. After a glass of champagne, Brie began to relax. "Sorry I keep freaking out. I'm not a scaredy-cat by nature, I swear."

Alec only shrugged. "Everyone is allowed to be afraid of something. You don't want to let fear rule you and stop you from living."

"Did you steal that from a fortune cookie?"

He leaned over and tapped the tip of her nose with his fingertip. "*Smart Alec,*" he whispered.

"Guilty," she chuckled. The alcohol was definitely working.

"So, you spent all day at the airport?" Alec asked.

"Yep. It about drove me crazy too."

"I can imagine." Alec finished the champagne. "Do you have someone coming to get you in Manchester?"

"My client has a private car that's supposed to be waiting for me. You?"

"I've ordered a car as well." He paused with his brows lowered and his lips pursed. "We could...have dinner, perhaps? Before you leave. Unless you need to be at your client's home by a certain time." He cleared his throat.

"I honestly would love to but...I don't want to upset my client. It would be unprofessional."

"Of course. Forget I asked." He reached for his brief-case, both the conversation and the offer were definitely over.

But Brie couldn't accept, even if she wanted to. The Countess had assured her she would have a late dinner prepared and Brie didn't want to be rude and miss it. The chance to write the book with the countess was a huge deal, not just for Brie but for her publisher, so she wasn't taking any chances.

There was a chime and the attendant at the front of the plane answered the telephone outside the cockpit. Brie sat up in her seat and nudged Alec.

"What's going on?"

"He's probably just telling her to turn off the seat-belt sign." Alec said but when the plane suddenly vibrated with the violent turbulence he frowned. The attendant sat back down in her chair and buckled in. "Well, I got that wrong."

"Oh God," Brie whispered.

"Ladies and gentlemen," the captain spoke over the speakers. "We've run into a heavy snowstorm which is hurting our visibility. We're over halfway to Manchester but I don't want anyone walking about the cabin until we—"

The plane jarred sharply and suddenly dipped. That free-fall feeling somersaulted Brie's stomach. She closed her eyes.

"It's going to be fine," Alec said. "It's just a bit of turbulence."

Just turbulence. Sure. For the next several minutes it felt like a cosmic hand was shaking the plane about. The attendant suddenly came over the intercom.

"Please prepare for a change in cabin pressure. Your masks will drop from above you. Please put them on."

"*What?*" Brie gulped, fear squeezing her throat painfully. She looked at Alec. He'd turned pale, but stayed calm.

The plane dipped again and this time it didn't steady out or come back up. The oxygen masks fell from the ceiling. She reached for hers, but her breath was already coming fast and far too shallow. Trying to grab the swaying device felt like trying to hit a piñata blindfolded.

Then Alec was there, his mask already secured, pulling a mask over her face and tightening the straps.

"You have air?" he asked as the rest of the passengers started to panic. She nodded frantically.

The captain's voice filled the cabin again. "Please remain calm. We are preparing for an emergency landing. Put on your masks and brace for impact."

Brie couldn't breathe, despite the oxygen pouring through the mask.

Oh God...

Alec gripped her hand hard and when they crouched down in the crash position, their eyes met. She saw something in his stare but couldn't place what it was. It was crazy, but it almost looked like...relief?

She had no time to think. No time to get to her phone and call her parents. No time left but this awful nightmare and Alec holding onto her hand...

4

The plane was crashing. Alec gripped Brie's hand tight. All he could think was he was going to die a coward because he was too afraid to make things right with his family.

The sides of the plane groaned around them as they lost altitude fast. Everything, from the seats to the luggage above their heads, was shaking violently. A few people were screaming but most were gasping into their masks. It was a sound that would haunt him for the rest of his life.

"Brace!" The pilot's voice sounded distant above the roar of the wind against the plane. Alec threw an arm over Brie's shoulders, shielding her as best he could before the world exploded around them.

He was still holding her in a death grip as the plane

skidded to a stop and all the passengers jerked back against their seats. The lights in the plane flickered and died. Dazed, his head pounding, Alec removed his oxygen mask and sucked in a breath. Ice cold air was coming in from the cracked window next to Brie. He could smell snow and...sheep? He lifted his arm off Brie who was still frozen, her eyes clamped shut.

"Hey..." he whispered soothingly, even though his own hands were shaking as he helped her sit up. "We're okay. We've landed." Though where exactly he couldn't be sure. He couldn't see anything outside except a wintry storm through the fogged window just beyond Brie's trembling shoulder.

"Al—Alec," She tried to burrow closer and he cupped her face. Her eyes were still shut tight.

"I need you to look at me, darling. Other passengers need help. Show me that you're all right."

Her dark lashes fanned up. At that moment, her lovely blue eyes were the most beautiful things he'd ever seen.

"I'm...I'm okay." He impulsively leaned in and pressed a kiss to her forehead before he unbuckled his seatbelt and stood. His legs wobbled as adrenaline surged in his system. The plane seemed intact, there was no gaping hole, but luggage had fallen from the overhead bins and scattered haphazardly around them.

He focused on helping those nearest him. The flight attendant came toward him, stumbling over the bags in the aisle, her face tight with worry.

"I can't get the door open…and I'm not feeling so well…" She bent over and vomited into the aisle.

Alec gently patted her back and escorted her into the nearest empty seat. "It's okay. Let me try." Brie came over to tend to the stewardess, and Alec headed up the aisle toward the cockpit.

A middle-aged man joined him at the front of the plane. "I'll help."

Alec jerked his head toward the cockpit door. "You think the pilots are all right?"

"I don't know." The man pounded a fist on the door. "Oy! Are you all right in there?"

"Yes!" A muffled shout came through the heavy metal door. "We're coming out."

Alec nodded at the main door. "Let's get this open." The two of them gripped the large red handle. They both strained as they cranked the door open. A gust of cold wind and snow filled the cabin.

The cockpit door opened, and pilots stumbled out.

"Is everyone okay?" One of the them asked. He was an older man, early fifties, Alec judged.

"I think so," Alex said, glancing back at the passengers on the plane. "Where are we?"

"Somewhere fifty miles south of Manchester. One of our engines had lost power. This field was our safest bet."

Alec walked back down the aisle, helping more passengers. When he got back Brie, she was still assisting the ill flight attendant.

"Anyone hurt?" Alec called out. There was a general shaking of heads much to Alec's relief.

"Has anyone called 999?" the man who helped Alec open the door asked.

"We radioed Manchester's airport right before we went down," the younger copilot said. "They're sending ambulances this way. But it's going to take them a while to reach us."

"Nicholas, find the extra blankets and pass them out." The pilot instructed his younger partner.

Alec helped them pass out blankets before he joined Brie at their seats.

"You all right?" He wrapped a blanket around her, making sure she was warm and then pulled her close to him and put an arm around her shoulders.

"Yeah...cold but okay. Are you?"

He nodded. He actually felt the farthest thing from okay, but he wasn't about to admit that.

It took nearly half an hour for the fire and rescue teams to arrive. Two of the passengers suffering from anxiety were taken to the hospital straightaway and the rest gave statements to the police while they were all examined by the emergency crews. A fireman standing outside in the snow whistled loudly so that everyone set their attention on him.

"There are a dozen homes in the area that have opened their doors to you, since the snow is making it hard to get anywhere. We'll be sending you off in pairs, so please, pair up."

Brie shyly clung to his side. "Can I stick with you?"

"Certainly." Alec kept his arm around her as they let the others in the group go ahead of them. When it was their turn, they were put into the back of a police vehicle and the officer drove them to a small cottage abutting a pasture. Sheep were huddled in massive clumps, sleeping against the side of a barn. The police cruiser lights lit up the house as the front door opened. A matronly woman with shoulder length gray hair wearing a heavy housecoat waved at them.

"That'll be Mrs. Fellers. She's a right nice lady," the officer said. "She'll take good care of you."

Alex helped Brie out of the car and helped the officer remove their luggage from the boot of the car. It had been a small mercy that they had been able to take their carry-on and checked baggage with them.

"You two will be all right. Call if you need any help

tomorrow. The airline will be in touch to file any claims you have."

Alec thanked the officer before heading inside. Brie was already warming up and chatting with Mrs. Fellers.

It was going to be a hell of a night and he still had to call his mother to explain. She was expecting him home tonight, and he didn't want her to worry.

He paused just in front of the kitchen, listening to their host put the kettle on while she talked to Brie. *Hello mum, I almost died in a plane crash.* Somehow, he didn't think that would help. For now, a white lie would have to do.

He took a moment to text his mother and father that his flight was canceled due to the weather and he would be there first thing in the morning. Then he straightened his shoulders and entered the kitchen.

BRIE WATCHED MRS. FELLERS BREW SOME TEA. SHE'D welcomed Brie inside, tutting and fretting as she regaled Brie with how the entire village of Cottonvale had been calling each other for the last hour while the police collected passengers from the flight, and what a miracle it was that nobody was seriously hurt.

"It's created quite the buzz, you know. It will be the

talk of Cottonvale for weeks. We never get visitors, not this far from Manchester." Mrs. Fellers turned to her with an empty teacup and set it down on the walnut wood kitchen table.

"Thank you," Brie said as the woman continued fussing over her.

"What you need is some nice chamomile tea and a warm bed." Mrs. Fellers added as Alec walked into the kitchen. "I'm sure your husband will be glad to rest."

"Oh he's..." She stopped abruptly and didn't correct Mrs. Fellers. "Yes, I'm sure he will."

"Welcome." Mrs. Fellers handed him a cup of tea too. "Cream and sugar, dearie?" She asked him.

"A bit of cream, thank you." He eased into a chair beside Brie. There was a look of weariness to his face that hadn't been there before.

"Did you call your family?" she asked.

"I sent a text. I told them my flight was canceled and I would be arriving in the morning. If I told them what truly happened, my whole family would be searching the snowdrifts for me."

"I should call my client," she paused. "Do you think I should tell her the same thing? I wouldn't want her to worry."

"If you think they would, then yes. I believe a little white lie is sometimes necessary." Alec glanced at her purse. "You need to borrow a phone? Roaming charges can be murder."

"I have an international data plan, but thanks." Brie looked at their host, who was putting some short bread cookies in a tin on the table. "Mrs. Fellers, I'm going to step into the hall to make a quick call. Thank you again for the tea."

"Happy to help, my dear." The woman turned to Alec, peppering him with questions about if they were hungry and wanted dinner.

Brie slipped into the hall and dialed the Countess of Merryvale's cell which she still couldn't believe she even had. But the countess had insisted on being easy to reach as they collaborated on the book together. Brie's nerves jumped as she listened to the phone ring.

"Hello?" the Countess answered.

"Lady Merryvale, it's Brie Honeyweather."

"Honestly, dear, I insist you call me Julia."

"Julia." Despite her insistence, it felt wrong to address her so casually. "My flight got canceled. I have a place to stay that's actually halfway between Manchester and Merryvale, all is good. I just won't be in until tomorrow morning."

"Text me your address and I'll have the car sent to you first thing in the morning."

"I think we're still a couple hours away. That's too far for someone to drive."

"Nonsense. We have an SUV with four-wheel-drive that can get through the snow and our driver, Mr. Baines, will be able to get you by ten AM."

"Yes, that would work. Thank you so much."

"It seems a dozen flights have been canceled due to the weather. I was lucky one of my sons arrived early, but my other seems to be running late as well. I'm hoping you'll be able to meet the whole family. Veronica and Thad are all settled and little Lyra loves Morgan, my younger son. You would never know Morgan wasn't a child by the way he acts when around children. He's wonderful with kids."

Brie laughed. "Well, to be fair, Lyra acts old for her age."

"And Morgan is too young." The countess chuckled. "Well, I should let you sleep. Call me if anything changes, and don't forget to text me your address."

"I will," Brie promised and hung up. She returned to the kitchen where Mrs. Fellers was toiling over a large pot on the stove and cutting up some potatoes and leeks.

"I know it's late, but you both must eat. Dinner will be ready in ten minutes, if you want to settle in upstairs."

Alec handed Brie the tea Mrs. Fellers had made for her. It was smooth and she tasted a hint of honey.

"Thank you, Mrs. Fellers. We'll be back down shortly." Alec nodded for Brie to go back into the hall. "If you take my briefcase, I'll carry the suitcases," he offered.

"Sure." She would have carried her own luggage, but she wasn't about to refuse the help. Her body still felt off, and part of her was still trembling from the whole ordeal.

She picked up her purse and backpack, along with Alec's briefcase as she watched Alec heft the two large suitcases and carry them upstairs ahead of her. She had to admit the rear view of the jeans he wore was mouth-watering. He gave her all sorts of wicked thoughts, ones she would feel bad about later. After everything she'd been through tonight, she deserved a little mental self-indulgence.

Alec navigated the narrow hall with ease despite the bulk of the suitcases, but he paused at the top, glancing in one room and another before he looked back at her in confusion.

"What's the matter?"

"Well…there's only one bedroom. This other room," he jerked his head to the room behind him. "Is the water closet."

"But there are two beds, right?"

He shook his head.

"One bed?" She clarified as he carried the suitcases into the bedroom. When she followed him inside, she saw there was indeed one bed, cleaned by the looks of it.

"Um... maybe she has a couch. One of us could..."

"No couch. I saw her living room. It had only a couple of armchairs."

Brie stared at the bed. "Okay, so we're both adults. We can share a bed. Without things...you know..."

"We can," Alec agreed, but she heard a distinct note of uncertainty in his voice.

"Which side would you like?" she asked. Brie did her best to act casual, but her heart was pounding at the thought of sharing a bed with this gorgeous man.

"By the door, but I can sleep on either side."

"That works for me." She set her purse down and he pushed his briefcase under the bed to give them room. The quilted coverlet and the rustic furnishings made the room feel warm and inviting, though perhaps a little too inviting.

They rejoined Mrs. Fellers in the kitchen, where two bowls of homemade potato and leek soup were waiting for them. The creamy hot soup was full of flavor and just eating it made Brie feel a lot calmer after everything that had happened.

"Now, you'll be wanting a hot shower or bath. There's a bath in the room upstairs. Towels are in the cupboards. If you think of anything else you need, just let me know. My room is down here on the first floor."

Once they were finished, Mrs. Fellers bid them good night and headed off to bed. Brie found the dishwasher and Alec cleaned the bowls and spoons. Once everything was loaded, she glanced at Alec.

"Do you mind if I have the first shower?"

"Not at all. I showered at my apartment between flights."

She retrieved her shower kit and a fresh change of clothes from her suitcase before heading into the bathroom. It was bigger than she expected, with a tub that had shower doors. She closed the door to the hall, stripped out of her clothes, and cranked the hot water on.

It took a moment for the water to heat, so she stood shivering and bare, with one hand beneath the cool spray testing for warmth. By the time she got inside, she was nearly shaking, but it wasn't at all from the cold. She tried to wash her hair and face and not think about the crash now that she was alone...but it was all she could see.

The look on Alec's face. The masks dropping down. The sound of the plane grinding against the ground.

She'd been unable to breathe as she waited for it to explode. As she waited for them to die. Then Alec... He'd covered her body with his and held her tight. He'd protected her.

He'd thought of someone other than himself. And when the plane crashed, she'd been so shellshocked she hadn't been able to help anyone at first. She'd been frozen, barely able to breathe, but he'd been helping others right from the start.

Brie crumpled to the floor of the shower, curling up under the hot spray and staying like that long after the water started to cool.

"Brie?" Alec's voice came from the other side of the door.

She snapped out of it, scrambling up and turning the water off. "Just a sec!" Quickly, she stepped out, wrapped a towel around her body, and hastily combed her wet hair with her fingers before she cracked the door open. Alec peered down at her through the slit of the door frame.

"Are you all right?" he asked, his eyes dark with worry. "You've been in there for over half an hour."

"Yeah, totally fine," she lied.

His gaze narrowed. "You've been crying."

"What? No, I haven't." She rushed to the counter to

peer at her reflection in the mirror. Her eyes were red. Had she been crying and didn't even realize it?

Alec shouldered his way into the bathroom. "Brie..."

She spun to face him. "No, I'm okay. I'm *really* okay." She held up a hand, but he caught it and pulled her close. Her eyes closed and she surrendered to the feel of being near him. She felt safe here. She didn't know how that was possible. They were basically strangers, yet she felt like as long as he held her, she didn't have to be afraid.

"How come you aren't falling apart?" she muttered miserably as he held her.

"I did that on the plane after the plane stopped sliding in the snow." He cupped the back of her head, massaging her scalp through the wet tendrils. "Men process adrenaline faster than women."

"What? That's BS." She burrowed closer to him.

"No, it's true. We have an immediate adrenaline rush to get through a battle, for example. Women have the same amount of adrenaline, but it doesn't kick in until much later and it lasts far longer. Women tend to react more calmly. They maintain strength and speed to collect the food and children before they escape to safety. But when you come down from the adrenaline, it's a lot harder than men do. My hands were shaking the second after the plane stopped. I just about fell over trying to walk down the aisle. I was already peaking from hormones and started coming down right as your rush started."

"You know, that sounds really sexist." Brie almost smiled with her words.

"It's science. It's actually sexist against men if you think about it. You have the advantage to get through something dangerous for a longer period of time than I do. We're treated like cannon fodder. Besides, I think you are handling the situation rather well. But you need to relax. Rest. It's the best way to get over this anxiety you're feeling." He nodded at her clothes. "Change and then let's sleep, all right?"

"Okay." Brie stepped back before Alec turned to leave her alone in the bathroom. She changed into her pajamas, dried her eyes and her hair as best she could.

Alec was already lounging in the bed wearing just a pair of flannel gray pajama pants when she came into the bedroom. He had his iPad out and was staring at the screen. He looked up from his tablet as he said, "Sorry, I didn't have a spare shirt, and I don't usually wear one to sleep. Does it bother you?"

His long, graceful fingers moved elegantly as he typed whatever he was working on. After a second, he closed the device and focused on her. God, all those sleek muscles and raw power. Even just sitting there he looked impressive. His suit had looked so good on him, but what lay beneath the clothes was so much better. She let out a little sigh and then realized he'd been talking.

"Hmmm?" She inwardly winced. "Sorry, what did you say?"

He chuckled. "I'll take that as a no." His laugh sent a delicious, intimate thrill through her. It was the sort of laugh that only a lover of this man would hear, a sound reserved for the bedroom. Brie responded instantly and had to fold her arms over her chest to hide her nipples hardening.

Alec set his iPad on the nightstand and pulled back the quilt and sheet. While she climbed into her side of the bed, he turned off the overhead light. Except for the dim light from the small lamp on the nightstand, darkness surrounded them. With a quick crank of the little switch on the lamp by his strong hands, that light died as well. It was nearly pitch black and incredibly quiet. All she heard was the wind whistling against the pair of windows opposite the bed.

Brie trembled, a chill filling her as she remembered the moment the plane had crashed in that field. Only now, in her mind, nothing was left but cold, snow-covered corpses. Fresh panic flared inside her and she let out a shaky sigh.

Alec rolled over to face her. "What's wrong?" His features were shadowy, like a dark prince from a realm of dreams.

"Sorry." She felt ridiculous for letting what *hadn't* happened upset her. "I'm just still...freaked out. I keep seeing us crash over and over."

Alec pressed closer. The heat of his body seeped into hers. When he draped a large arm over her, she couldn't deny how much she liked the feeling of him holding her. This intimacy was one of the things she missed about marriage. So much time had passed since she let herself feel like this. Would it really be so bad to let this man hold her and make her feel protected, even just for a night?

"You don't need to be afraid. You're safe tonight, all right?" His tone was soft and soothing.

She gently pressed her palm against his cheek. A faint scruff met her skin. He must have showered early, because a beard was already coming in. That barely-there beard on a man's face always got to her in the best way. Their gazes met as he slowly turned to kiss her palm. A pang of arousal hit her so hard she had to clamp her thighs together.

And just like that they both knew what could happen...what they both *wanted* to happen. Fire raced between them as he kissed the inside of her wrist. Now was the time to stop, to put a stop to this, but she didn't want to.

"Alec," she spoke his name in a whisper. "If we do this, it's a one-time thing, right? I'm not looking for a relationship."

"Neither am I," he murmured. "But I think we both need this."

"Okay." She leaned in, but a new reality crashed down on her. "Shit. Do you have a condom?"

"Fuck. No, I don't usually carry them."

He started to pull away, but she curled an arm around the back of his neck. "I have an IUD and I'm clean."

Alec blew out a soft breath. "I'm clean as well. Last checkup was a month ago and I haven't had sex since then."

"So...we're good?" She was done with talking, done worrying. She just needed *him*.

"We're good." He rolled over, pressing her into the soft mattress. It creaked slightly as his weight settled. She'd forgotten how good it felt to have a hard-male body on top of her like this. His warm lips coasted down her neck in light playful caresses.

Alec pinned her palms on either side of her head as he kissed her, taking his time to settle between her thighs. She wore only a pair of panties under polka dot pink and black silk boxers with a button up nightshirt, but the way he was kissing her, she felt *naked*... Naked and desperate for what the hard length of him promised.

The lust she'd been fighting to ignore ever since they'd met was fast becoming a devouring obsession. Even the simple act of him kissing her while gently restraining her was thrilling beyond words. She was wet and aching by the time he flicked his tongue against hers and released her wrists. He slid down her body, pulling her shorts and panties off before tossing them out of reach.

"Unbutton your shirt." His voice gruff and sexy, but the command was quiet so as not to wake their host downstairs.

She frantically pulled at the buttons, her chest heaving with excitement as she parted the shirt. He nudged her legs apart and kissed his way up one of her calves before reaching her mound.

"Touch yourself while I taste you," he order.

Brie reached for one breast. Her face flooded with heat as she rolled her nipple. The second his warm breath fanned over her sensitive mound she whimpered with desperate desire. When he licked her slit, she almost screamed at the explosion of sensations.

"Oh, my Go—"

Alec covered her mouth with one of his hands and kissed a path back up her body.

"You have to be quiet, or else I can't do terribly bad, wicked things to you. Nod if you understand."

She nodded. Girl, did she nod.

"Good girl," he said and moved his hand from her lips.

She could see the shadowy outline of his smirk from the sliver of moonlight coming in from the windows. He bent his head to nuzzle her chest and sucked the tip of one of her nipples into his mouth. He tugged on the peak until she was biting her lip and squirming. Taking that as a sign, he moved back down between her legs, only this time she was ready when he flicked his tongue against her wet folds. She swallowed the cry of excitement that tried to escape as he devoured her. Her legs were shaking violently as her climax came closer, so close she could feel it just out of her reach.

He slid up her body, his muscled form slipping between her parted legs and used one hand to position himself before he eased inside of her.

"Fuck, you're so tight..." he groaned. "Almost too tight..." He claimed her, inch by inch, until he was so deep that their hips collided. The feeling of fullness, almost to the point of discomfort, was overwhelming.

In the last few years, she'd forgotten what it felt like

to belong to someone else in the dark, where shadows hid all but one's passions. Alec made love slow and hard, owning her with every deep thrust. He braced his forearms on either side of her head, trapping her with his strength. He obliterated every last bit of fear from the crash with his devastating lips, hot enough to burn the world down. Lips that made her remember fleetingly how she'd once felt before and had foolishly mistaken those feelings for love. She knew better now. This was raw, animal lust and physical satisfaction, nothing more. But she fully intended to enjoy it as such.

When her climax hit, she welcomed the glittering stardust against the backs of her eyelids. She clung to Alec, her nails scraping his shoulders as his pleasure continued to roll in endless tidal waves while he thrust inside her a dozen more times, harder and faster until he filled her womb. He gasped against her neck and his muscles relaxed as he eased down over her.

A sudden sense of loss made her cling to him even harder. It was over. He seemed to sense her thoughts, just like he had on the plane.

"I'm not going anywhere tonight," he murmured in her ear. "I'm yours." It was as though he'd known exactly what she'd needed to hear most, and more importantly, meant it.

She relaxed beneath him, allowing her hold on his

shoulder to loosen. He eased out of her and reposition ed himself to lay beside her. After he lifted the blankets around them, he pulled her into the curve of his body, spooning her into a perfect position. She held onto his arm around her waist, but the exhaustion won out and her eyes drifted shut.

5

Dawn broke through the windows, the sun reflecting off the heavy dusting of snow that had gathered in the corners of the windowpanes. Alec squinted against the light and shifted in bed. For moment he forgot where he was before it all came back in violent flashes.

The crash, the cold, the snowy village, Brie crying at the bathroom door.

She'd looked so young, so vulnerable and raw. The sight of her like that had nearly ripped his heart out. The last thing he wanted was to hurt her or take advantage of her. But when she'd touched him with a trembling hand, it had shattered his control.

Yet he didn't regret one bloody second of it. It had

been one of the best nights he'd ever had, and he wasn't sure if that was a good thing or a bad thing.

She needed me, and I needed her. We both needed to feel alive after what we'd been through.

Yet a small little voice in the back of his mind whispered that what happened wasn't just some affirmation of life, but maybe something more. Still, he had no time to date, and she'd been adamant last night that the last thing she wanted was a relationship. Today they would go their separate ways and never see each other again. Until then...

Alec rolled over to curl his body around hers. She was soft and naked, like him; the way he liked most to wake up in the morning next to a woman.

"Five more minutes..." Brie burrowed closer to him and her delectable bottom settled against his very hard cock. Her drowsy mutter was adorable.

"Do that again and I might roll you beneath me," he whispered in her ear.

She smiled at that. If she'd been a cat, she'd have purred and rubbed herself against him invitingly. For now, he didn't bother to roll her beneath him. Instead, he lifted her leg, opening her up and stroking her folds with slow, teasing, erotic touches. When she was dripping and wide awake, he slid into her from behind. In response, she moaned softly and clutched at his arm around her waist.

They made love quietly, slowly this time, and he burned every second of it into his mind. The way motes of dust swirled in eddies above her head, glinting in tiny sparkles. The way her dark hair glowed in the morning light, and how the hidden russet strands were illuminated between the darker chocolate tones. He didn't want this to end, but as she climaxed in a soft gasp, he was compelled to join her only seconds later. As he held her from behind, he faced the reality that in a few hours, this would be over.

They lay together for a long time before he let her slip away. She retrieved her clothes from the floor and rushed into the bathroom across the hall. Alec rolled onto his back and stared at the ceiling. In a few hours he'd be on his way to Merryvale for the holidays with his family, and even though Thad would be there, he was not looking forward to it at all.

When Brie returned, freshly showered, he dragged himself out of bed and fetched a shower kit to take his own. As he washed away Brie's scent, he knew he was going to miss it. Once he was done and dressed, he found her downstairs in the kitchen with Mrs. Fellers, who had made scrambled eggs and tea.

"You have a good sleep, dears?" she asked them.

"Yes, thank you. We really appreciate you letting us stay the night." Brie smiled warmly at the older woman. Alec was fascinated with the way her smile lit up her face. Had any woman he'd been with before ever had a smile like that? He honestly couldn't remember.

"How far do you need to travel?" Mrs. Fellers asked.

"About two hours for me." Alec glanced at Brie, still curious as to who her client was. If it was anyone noteworthy, he would bet anything that his parents would know them.

"Same for me, I think." Brie helped their host with the dishes and Alec went upstairs to retrieve their suitcases. His hired car arrived minutes after he'd brought all their luggage down into the front hall.

"Goodbye, Mrs. Fellers." He hugged the elder woman who blushed and patted his back. Then he turned to Brie who was waiting for him with bright eyes.

"So, this is it," she said with a shaky smile.

"Bet you'll be glad to be rid of me, eh?" he joked.

She bit her lip and nodded. "Definitely. You're such a jerk."

"Only with the *truly* annoying ladies." She laughed at the way he said that. The teasing kept their parting nearer to sweet than sorrow.

"Do you...?" He wasn't sure what he wanted to say

and perhaps it was a mistake, but he slid a business card in her hand. "In case you need it." He spun and headed down the snowy steps of the cottage and into the waiting SUV. He didn't dare look back.

As the hired car pulled away from the cottage, he dug around his briefcase for his iPad but his fingertips bumped against the book Brie had let him keep. He pulled it out and stared at the title: *No Rest for the Wicked*. He opened it to the first page. This was going to be ridiculous, but it seemed more appealing than reading the paper online, at least for the next couple of hours.

The rest of the trip was a blur as he got sucked into the story of the dashing rogue pirate Dominic and his feisty English love who'd hid aboard his captured vessel dressed as a cabin boy hoping to find out what happened to her father.

"We're here, sir," the driver announced, pulling Alec out of the story. He had only handful of chapters left, which meant he'd have to find time to finish the book later. He'd been rather surprised by how invested he'd become in the characters and the plot. There'd been a good mystery and a fair amount of sea battles, plus a loyal friendship between the hero and his best friend. And the sex...well...he'd made fun of Brie for it, but the scenes had certainly been good.

He leaned forward and peered through the front window, taking in the grand castle-like structure ahead of him. The lawns were covered in snow and the fifty-foot Cyprus trees, that even during the summer still carried the scent of winter, were shivering with an icy wind. They resembled a huddle of old men in dark green snowy capes.

The tan stones of Merryvale were a bright gold in the winter sunlight and numerous windows flashed as the SUV drove up the gravel drive to stop in front of the tall oak doors of the main entrance.

I'm home.

Alec's heart gave a painful jolt. Memories fought their way to the surface. *He and Morgan racing down the hill, sleds in hand, with coats and caps firmly fixed as they hollered like wild puppies. His grandfather, looking on from the top of the nearest hill, waving at them.*

That had been the last time he'd seen his grandfather alive. He'd died of a stroke that afternoon in his study on Christmas day. Every Christmas after that was shadowed by the familiar pain. Alec looked away from the house, forcing himself to push the memories of his grandfather away.

The front door opened, and a trio of dogs sprinted onto the snowy driveway, barking like mad. Morgan, Alec's younger brother, stood there grinning widely.

Alec got out and helped the driver with his bags. The dogs were all around him now, jumping at his heels. A dark colored English Springer Spaniel danced excitedly and sniffed his suitcase.

"Hello Copper." He gave the dog a ruffle of his silky ears. A male white and brown bulldog, Yogi, gave a series of snuffling huffs as he toddled around, inspecting the luggage. "Yogi, old boy." Alec chuckled as he and the bulldog stared at one another. The last dog, a tall black English lab, wagged her tail and followed the driver around.

"Pepper, come." He called to the lab. She joined him, resting her head against his leg and gazing up at him in adoration.

"At least the dogs are happy to see you." Morgan snickered as he came down and embraced Alec.

"The dogs always did have better taste in people than you." He laughed and smacked his brother's back before he handed his driver his fare and a tip. Morgan grabbed Alec's suitcase in a surprising show of sibling kindness. "I'm not dying, Morgan."

"Don't be too sure about that. Mum found out about the crash. Dad had your flight info and checked this morning. Mum was making tea when he told her about it. She broke her best china teapot."

"The blue and white Sadler one?" Alec winced as Morgan nodded.

"Well, it was nice knowing you, Alec," Morgan chuckled, but then after a moment, his gaze turned serious. "Is it true no one died? Dad wanted to call but he knew it would only upset Mum."

"Everyone was fine. A few people had some panic attacks, but it was mostly just a good scare." He didn't want to think about the flight or the crash because, mostly because it reminded him of Brie.

He and Morgan stepped inside and he set his attaché case down on the floor. The dogs ran past him, with Yogi huffing and snuffling as he brought up the rear. The dogs lead the way into the drawing room where his family gathered in private when the house was open for tours to the public. The house was closed over the Christmas holidays, but it was still an old habit to retreat to the drawing room at this time of day. The red painted walls were enhanced by a gold crown molding he'd always thought looked like some baroque period palace. The furnishings, however, were modern, with leather sofas and comfortable plush armchairs.

"Is that you, Alec?" Julia's voice was a slightly higher pitch than normal as she leapt from her writing desk in the corner.

He opened his arms and she hugged him. "Hello, mum."

"Hello mum? *Hello mum*? That's all you have to say after you almost *died* last night and didn't tell us? "Flight was *cancelled*..." she scoffed.

"Well, technically it was cancelled," Alec countered. "Just...after we took off."

"Don't be cute with me. It doesn't suit you." His mother spun around, scowled, and turned to his father who had abandoned his newspapers and stood from his position by the couch. "He gets that from you. I'm sure of it."

"I didn't want you to worry. I'm fine, mum. I'm here, aren't I?"

"The boy has a point, Jules," his father said. Byron gently pried his mother off him and embraced Alec.

"I'm sorry, Alec. I'm just a bit rattled. First you and then Ms. Honeyweather. It's all so dreadful!"

Alec went rigid. "Ms...Honeyweather?"

"Oh right, I hadn't had a chance to tell you, since you *never* call me." Julia shot a judgmental look that only a mother was capable of.

"Tell me what?"

"Remember that I've always said I wanted to write a history of Merryvale?"

He had a terrible feeling he wouldn't like what his mother was about to say.

"So, I decided to do it. A book about our Christmas traditions here at Merryvale. I've even hired a lovely... What's she called, dear?" Julia looked at his father for help. "Not a script doctor, those are for movies."

"A ghostwriter." Her father supplied as he scratched Yogi's head. The bulldog gazed up at Byron with devotion. The two were almost inseparable. Copper and Pepper tended to love everyone equally, but Yogi was the earl's dog through and through.

"Yes, Ms. Honeyweather. She's an American. My New York publisher hired her to help me give the book that literary flair." Her mother's smile soon faded. "Ms. Honeyweather's flight was canceled due to the storm. She should be here shortly. We sent a driver to pick her up.."

Alec was never more thankful that his job had trained him to master his facial expressions. He'd had a one night stand with the woman his mother had hired to write a book for her. A woman who would be spending the holidays here with him at the house.

His mother looked at him expectantly. "Well, aren't you excited for me?"

"That's wonderful, mother." He cupped her shoulders and gave her a kiss on her forehead.

She raised a brow. "You're not at all impressed?"

"I am. It's just been a long couple of days, that's all." He looked at Morgan and his father. "I think I'll just settle in and be down for tea in half an hour."

"Of course. Go on then," his mother encouraged. Alec left them and went into the hall. Copper, the spaniel, followed dutifully at his heels.

"Alec, wait." His brother caught up with him at the foot of the large staircase. They were only two years apart in age, but it often felt like decades given how different their personalities were. Morgan was a barrister, but despite the serious nature of his profession, he was charming and beloved by all. He was everything Alec wasn't.

Even as the eldest, Alec had somehow felt separated from his family because of how he'd handled his grandfather's death. Morgan constantly teased him for being the black sheep of the family. He'd all but abandoned them once he was old enough to make his own way in life.

"Are you really all right, Alec? I mean with the whole plane thing? I didn't mean to make light of it. You know how I am. Serious stuff scares the bloody hell out of me."

Alex smiled ruefully at his brother. "I know." They handled grief and fear so very differently. Morgan indulged in gallows humor. Alec buried it and walked away from anything that could drag it back to the surface.

"Well, if you need to talk…" Morgan offered.

"I'll be sure to talk to someone else," Alec teased, but then he laid a hand on his shoulder. "Thanks, Morgan."

"Thad and Veronica are in the blue suite; in case you want to see them before tea. Their daughter is so adorable."

Alec skated his hand along the mahogany banister, remembering his grandfather straddling him over it, whispering the secrets of how best to ride the banister down to the bottom.

The previous Earl of Merryvale hadn't been the stereotypical stiff, grumpy, old British man who harrumphed at boisterous children and drank too much brandy. Walter had been warm, loving, and adventurous. The lingering scent of fine cigars had only added to his charm. Every room at Merryvale held a beautiful, yet starkly painful memory of Walter. It was why coming home hurt so much.

Alec followed the hall on the right, where most of the guestrooms were located, and tried not to think of how Brie would soon be staying in one of these.

Then he chuckled as he realized she was going to

panic when she found him here and discovered who he was. He would wager anything she would freak out, but there was no way he could have known. She'd refused to tell him who her client was, and his mother had only just told him about hiring a ghostwriter.

Alec couldn't deny that part of him was excited to see her again, even if it was a bad idea given how he'd felt far too attached after what they'd shared following the crash. There was an undeniable pull, a longing for something more than one night and he knew it would be hard to resist. He couldn't afford a relationship, not now, not with his job.

They joked at the office about installing a fake graveyard for the tombs of their lost relationships, but the demanding life of an investment banker was no laughing matter. It often meant sleeping and showering at the office, no family dinners, no birthday parties with the kids, or wedding anniversary dinners. People in his line of work didn't care about or want these things. Neither did Alec.

Yet he knew with alarming certainty that his night with Brie had sown a seed of doubt about his life's choices. And he couldn't afford to doubt himself, not at such a pivotal time in his career. He paused in front of the blue suite with its two connected bedrooms, and knocked.

Thad's voice came from the other side of the door. "Just a minute." Then another shout came half a second later. "No, wait!" The door flung open and a girl around six years old shot out in the hall, colliding with Alec.

"Oof!" Alec clutched his stomach and stumbled back.

"Sorry, sir!" The girl gasped.

"That you, Alec? I was too busy chasing this monkey around the room." Thad appeared in the open doorway, and pretended to frown at the little girl which made her giggle. "Lyra, this is Alec, Morgan's older brother."

"*You're* Morgan's older brother?" the girl asked in excitement. It was clear by the way he said Morgan's name that the man was her own personal hero.

"Er, yes. Hello." Alec offered his hand and the girl shook it with solemn respect.

"Sorry for running into you, sir. I was excited to go sledding. Mr. Grange said he knew the best spots."

"Indeed, he does," Alec agreed. Mr. Grange was the Estate's groundskeeper.

Lyra looked hopefully toward Thad. "Can I go now, dad?"

Thad grinned and jerked his head at the girl to indicate she was free to leave. Lyra took off running down the hall.

"To be that young again," Alec chuckled.

Thad smiled warmly in agreement as he watched the girl vanish down the stairs. Then he called into the room behind him, "Veronica, Alec's here."

Alec had only met Veronica once, a year ago when he had some free time while in Chicago. They'd come in from Chicago to meet him.

Veronica joined Thad at the door and embraced him in a warm hug. "Alec!"

"You keeping him in line?" Alec asked her.

"Trying." Veronica laughed. "Did you see your parents yet? I'm afraid we've all heard about the emergency landing by now."

"Thank God you're not calling it a crash. Everyone else is acting like I rose from the ashes like a phoenix," Alec muttered.

"Well, it's a scary thing. Veronica just got off the phone with her friend. She was on your flight, too. Maybe you met her? Brie Honeyweather? She's going to work on your mum's holiday book."

"I...did meet her, actually. I had no idea she was working with mum. I only knew she was a writer."

"Is she okay? Brie is terrified of flying. She sounded calm on the phone just now, but she sometimes holds her anxiety inside until it gets to be too much and explodes."

"She was shaken, but we had the night to calm down." Alec assured Veronica. "The passengers were taken to local village homes close to where we landed. She was fine." So, Brie was Veronica's friend and he was Thad's. To think that their two different paths had been on a slow moving collision course this whole time was unnerving.

"What a relief," Veronica sighed. "I want her to be relaxed when she meets the countess." Her eyes glinted with mischief. "I've been talking to your mum and we both think she and Morgan might be a good fit."

"Morgan?" Alec choked on his brother's name. "Fit for what?"

"To date, naturally." Veronica grinned, and Alec could see why Thad fell for her. She was gorgeous, inside and out. But for that one moment, he didn't like her one bit. Morgan and Brie? No, absolutely not. They wouldn't get along at all.

"Morgan is so fun and charming. Brie needs that after her divorce," Veronica explained.

"Divorce?" Alec's breath tightened. She hadn't mentioned an ex-husband, not that it should matter. That's why they were an *ex* in the first place. They didn't owe each other dating histories. Still, he was glad she hadn't told him.

"Brie doesn't like to talk about it. She got married

young, like twenty-something, to her college sweetheart. And they got divorced at twenty-four. It's been five years and she still hasn't opened her heart up. I really think Morgan can show her how fun romance can be again."

"I don't think Morgan is a good choice," Alec said with his best poker face.

"Don't be silly. He's perfect. I'm not saying she should marry him, but he'd be good for her. Remind her not to give up looking for Mr. Right." Veronica retrieved her coat from the bed and kissed Thad's cheek. "I should go make sure Lyra doesn't bother the groundskeeper."

The moment Alec and Thad were alone, Thad crossed his arms and grinned.

"What?" Alec growled.

"You...you met Brie and you like her."

"I did meet Brie, and she's tolerable."

"Methinks you doth protest too much. You don't want her to date Morgan. That means you want to."

"I don't," Alec insisted, despite the bitter taste of the lie upon his tongue. "I just don't wish the fate of dating Morgan upon any poor woman. You know what he's like. He'll charm them into falling in love with him, and then walk away and break their hearts. He's not like me. The women I've hooked up with know going in that there's no expectation of relationship or love."

Thad slapped his shoulder. "You know...you've never worried about any of the other ladies Morgan's dated before. Why is this woman different?"

"She isn't," Alec could hear the lie as clearly as Thad could.

His friend chuckled wryly. "You can't lie to yourself forever. When she gets here, you'd better make a move, or your mum will be planning a wedding to Morgan before Brie goes back home."

Alex's hands curled into fists as they headed down the stairs for tea, but he vowed not to get involved. Maybe Veronica was right. Maybe Morgan would be good for her if she was just trying to get back on her feet dating-wise. If Brie liked Morgan, that was her business.

Wasn't it?

rie hugged Mrs. Fellers goodbye after the older lady extracted a promise from her to stay in touch. As she slid into the back seat of the SUV sent for her by the Countess of Merryvale, she realized she was sad to leave the smiling, waving, older lady. But as the little cottage vanished from view, she settled back and tried to relax. Tried.

In reality, Brie spent the two-hour drive staring out of the window, a slight frown on her forehead as she became increasingly lost in thoughts of Alec, and what had happened the night before.

She kept remembering the way he'd taken away the fear and uncertainty she felt from the plane crash. She'd been lost in passion, lost in him, and it had been amazing—life altering. He'd been gentle and strong at all the right times. He'd mastered her body with ease, yet she hadn't felt used or cheap. She'd felt valued and cherished with every kiss. She'd liked the hint of his playful dominating side, too. She flushed even now just thinking about it.

Her fingertips brushed over his business card. She hadn't even looked at it. She'd just tucked it into her coat pocket and left it there. The temptation to text him was strong, but that wouldn't be wise. Long distance relationships with a workaholic didn't last. It had been the final nail in the coffin for her and Preston's marriage.

She'd woken one day and realized she hadn't missed him at all after he'd moved to Manhattan for a better job. She was supposed to be packing up their house and prepare it for selling so she could move into their new apartment with him. But that morning, when she'd rolled over in bed and her hand fell against the bare pillow beside her, she hadn't felt empty. Hadn't felt...*anything*. She'd gone on about her day and it wasn't until lunch time when she realized she hadn't thought of Preston, not even once.

When they'd first dated, there had been such an intensity to everything—every look, every touch, every kiss. Even their text messages had been full of fire and life. But after four years, things had gone cold. They didn't fight, but maybe that was the problem. Neither of them had cared enough to fight about anything anymore.

She'd come to believe that maybe love didn't exist in the way she'd always thought of as a girl. Lust faded over time. Passion burned out. So, what was left? Would anything ever be left for her with another man? Was she doomed never to know what others seemed to when it came to happy relationships?

You won't see him again. Everything will be fine. You'll go back to Chicago and forget everything.

But she wouldn't forget.

As the SUV's tires ground over a snowy gravel drive, Brie glimpsed the tall proud edifice of Merryvale Court. The snow clouds had vanished, allowing bright winter sun to reflect off the white lawns.

"We're here," the driver announced, looking at Brie in the rearview mirror.

"It's beautiful," Brie said as the car stopped in the driveway.

"If you love it now, just wait till the spring. Everything is full of color then."

Brie removed a small notebook from her purse and began jotting down notes about the building's high silhouette on the sloping hill and the way a wooded path around the left of the house seemed to be guarded by the tallest cedar trees she'd ever seen.

The things those trees must have seen. She could imagine them two hundred years before, the trees' trunks thin, their stature small. Children's hands running about the trunks as they played games. The call of a horn and the thrill of a fox hunt...

A hundred years ago, the convalescing soldiers from the Great War would have looked upon their green boughs and dreamt of the days before trenches and the fog of war.

These trees had witnessed history. They had lived through night bombings and sweltering summers to the bitterest dry winters. They were a testament to the house and the family who lived within. What would these trees witness in the centuries to come?

The tall walnut wood front doors of Merryvale Court opened, and a couple emerged. Brie assumed it was the Earl of Merryvale and his wife. The Earl, Byron Halston, was over six feet tall, with dark hair and soft brown eyes. He was handsome and refined, but his smile promised warmth and kindness. Julia, Brie's official client, was a golden-haired beauty, tall and slender with glowing, ageless skin. There was something about her that tugged at Brie's memory.

"Brie, my dear." Julia separated from Byron to embrace her as though they were already old friends.

"It's so nice to meet you in person." Brie tried not to gush in excitement.

"I feel the same. Byron, come join us." She waved her husband over.

"My lord," Brie nodded, feeling like she should curtsy.

"Byron, please," he corrected. "We aren't too terribly formal these days, are we?" He gave his wife an almost bashful grin.

"Only during certain social engagements," Julia laughed and linked her arm through Brie's. "Come inside and let me show you around. Then we'll have tea."

Brie stepped into the Court's entry hall and gasped. Glowing garlands decorated with silver, red, and green ornaments draped the rails of the grand staircase. A massive Christmas tree was in the room just beyond.

"That's the salon. It's the largest and tallest room," Julia explained. Brie tipped her head back to stare up at the massive and perfectly-decorated tree.

Candles were scattered throughout the house and clusters of poinsettias graced various tables. Holly trimmed the tops of every doorway. It was an indoor winter wonderland. Brief half expected to see it start snowing inside, such was the magic of this place.

"This is so beautiful. Do you mind if I take a few pictures? I don't want to miss any details."

"Not at all." Julia looked proudly around the salon.

Brie dug her phone out of her purse and started taking pictures.

"Look out!" someone yelled. A moment later, a herd of panting beasts rushed into the room. Brie's legs were knocked out from under her. She waved her arms wildly as she gasped and started to fall, only to stop in mid-air. A pair of strong arms had caught her and helped get her standing straight. She turned to thank whoever had caught her and gasped.

"Well, hello there." He grinned and her knees wobbled.

It was another devilishly handsome British man. *What is in the water here?*

"Hi," Brie murmured in a daze at the brilliance of his charming smile.

"Oh heavens, Morgan, don't let the dogs do that!" Julia exclaimed.

"Morgan? You're Julia's son?"

"Yes." Morgan smiled as her stomach flipped. He smiled like Alec did.

God, I do have a type. Sexy British blond men with gorgeous smiles.

"I'm Brie."

"It's lovely to meet you." Now that she was steady, he bent to ruffle the furry heads of the three dogs bouncing around at their feet. He was tall and had the same burnished gold hair as his mother yet his face favored his father. He wore a dark maroon cable knit sweater, gray trousers, and black boots. Again, she was struck with that odd sense of familiarity from this complete stranger which made no sense at all.

"Sorry about the mutts," Morgan teased as he squished up the Bulldog's face. "This is Yogi." The bulldog licked its nose and sniffled, his stump of a tail wiggling.

"Yogi? Like a yoga teacher?"

"Like the bear from the American cartoons. He eats everything and he *will* steal your pic-i-nic basket." Morgan turned to the tall, but dainty, black lab. "This is Pepper. She is the lady of the house. My father expected her to be a hunting dog, but she found her way into their bed one night and he couldn't find it in his heart to keep her with the other hunting hounds."

"And this one?" Brie knelt and patted the head of the chocolate-colored spaniel.

"Copper. He's the general, keeping everyone in line,

or tries to." Morgan stroked Copper's ears and then looked up at her. "Do you like dogs, Brie?"

"I love them. I never really had one when I was younger. My ex-husband was allergic and after we divorced, I just sort of forgot I could get one, you know?"

It was odd. This was the first time she really talked about Preston to a stranger. Maybe it was because Morgan made her think of Alec and all the things she wanted to whisper deep into the night, the secrets she'd wanted to unbury and let go of. But there hadn't been time and she hadn't been brave enough. Still, she wondered if perhaps her chance meeting with Alec had opened her up to the possibility of letting her guard down around men again. Maybe that was why talking to Morgan was easier than she'd expected.

"They're really sweet." She patted the bulldog before the trio of dogs sprinted off across the salon and out a door on the opposite end as if summoned by an invisible master.

"So, you ready to help mum write her book?" Morgan asked.

"Not yet. I need to sit down with her and write out all the traditions, anecdotes, family stories, and recipes."

Morgan's warm eyes twinkled. "You *have* met my

mum, right? The woman doesn't know how to sit still for more than five minutes. She'll drag you from here to sundry and back in half an hour."

Morgan's head shifted, looking at something above and behind her.

"Ah, there you are. Been wondering if you'd ever come down." Morgan turned to Brie and winked. "Care to meet the black sheep of our family?"

"Black sheep?" Brie was curious to see who Morgan was talking about. She turned, only to have the wind knocked out from her lungs.

"This is my older brother, Alec. Workaholic. Holiday hater. Only begrudgingly spends time with his beloved family. The rest of us Halstons adore family and the holidays. Ergo, he's the black sheep."

He was here. At Merryvale court. Standing just a few feet away from her.

Oh. My. God.

Alec was a Halston. Alec was Julia's eldest child...

I just slept with my client's son.

"Alec, this is mum's ghostwriter, Brie Honeyweather."

"We've met." Alec's hazel eyes were locked on Brie. She felt trapped...or maybe a little transfixed. But she couldn't move as he came toward her and held out his hand. "It's nice to see you again, Ms. Honeyweather."

"Y-you too," she replied, placing her hand in his. It felt like a lifetime ago that they'd parted ways, but it had only been a few hours. She realized instantly that she'd missed him. Was it even possible to miss a stranger?

"Hold on a moment, you've met?" Morgan pushed his way between them. "How?"

"We flew together from Chicago and London, then London to Manchester."

Morgan's face went pale. "So, she was on the plane when...?"

"What?" Julia had returned to them just in time to hear their conversation. "Brie was on the plane that crashed? I thought you told me your flight was canceled?"

Brie's face flamed. "I didn't want you to worry. I was fine, really."

Julia looked horrified. "You could've died! You need a cup of tea, *right now*. We can do the tour later." Julia gently dragged her away from the brothers who were whispering to each other as Brie and Julia left the salon.

"To think what could've happened," Julia muttered. "It was a miracle no one was hurt."

"Really, I'm okay. I swear." She was far more concerned about what the Countess would think if she knew that Alec had slept with her.

"This way." Julia escorted her to a drawing room and set her down in a chair by the fire. After a few minutes, a maid set a tray down for Julia who poured two cups of tea.

"What happened after the plane landed in the field? We heard passengers stayed in houses nearby."

"Yes, we were driven to homes nearby. It really wasn't a big deal. I stayed with a lovely woman named Mrs. Fellers."

"Oh, well good." The Countess didn't seem all that convinced Brie was all right but was willing to take her word for it. "And you met my eldest, Alec?"

"Yes," Brie replied with caution. Since she hadn't had a chance to talk with Alec, she wasn't sure how much she ought to reveal about their interactions, or whether they needed to get their stories straight.

Julia's face paled slightly at Brie's confirmation of meeting Alec. "I must apologize."

Brie didn't understand. "For what?"

"Well," Julia smoothed her dark blue, knee-length skirt as she stared at her hands. "Alec is...not quite as charming as Morgan, and he could hardly have given you the best impression of our family. He despises Christmas. It's a miracle he's even here this year. If it wasn't for Thad and Veronica..."

"He knows Thad and Veronica?"

"Oh, yes. Didn't Veronica tell you? I met her through Thad, of course, who I've known for years now. He and Alec met when Thad attended Cambridge University during a few summers in college. It was Thad who convinced Alec to come home to visit for Christmas this year."

Brie took a sip of tea, relishing the smokey Earl Grey taste and a hint of sugar and milk, just the way she liked. But her thoughts kept coming back around to Alec.

"So, Alec doesn't like Christmas?"

Julia's gaze softened as she looked out the window at the snow blanketed grounds. "He used to *love* Christmas. He used to love Merryvale. But..." She paused, her voice a little husky with emotion. "His grandfather, Walter, died of a stroke on Christmas when he was a child and everything changed. He was hurt and angry. Neither Byron nor I could reach him. He was incredibly close to Walter, you see. They shared a special bond, and when he died, it left my little boy brokenhearted." Julia met Brie's gaze. "A mother can't protect her child from everything. We strive valiantly to do so, but it's impossible. Death is a part of life, part of growing up, but it's never easy to come to terms with. I believe it came too soon for Alec. I know coming here must hurt him, but this is his *home.* It will be his to live in and care for when Byron and I are gone. I don't..." Julia's eyes were glittering with tears now. "I don't know how to bring my son back, the son I loved and lost. The man you've met? He's not the sweet, open-hearted child we raised."

Brie reached a hand toward Julia's knee. "Maybe being here and remembering the history of this place will remind him of who he used to be."

The Countess wiped her eyes and smiled as she tried to hide her pain. "Perhaps you are right. Finish your tea and I'll start by telling you about our biggest Christmas tree."

ALEC STOOD NEXT TO MORGAN IN THE MAIN SALON AS THEY stared up at the twenty-eight-foot spruce that reached the gallery above. The salon was a square room that went up two floors with overhanging walkways and balconies that overlooked the ground floor below. At Christmas, the room transformed into an oasis of green and gold. Their family coat of arms, along with other various crests, were placed on the stone balconies above and garlands hung down over the railings. Alec had forgotten how incredible Merryvale looked at

Christmas time, which only made it more painful to be here.

"So, you and Ms. Honeyweather are acquainted, are you?"

"We sat on the same plane, so yes," Alec replied without showing any emotion. He could count on Morgan to make trouble if he thought it would be amusing. Better to stop his little brother before he got started.

"Come now. I'm not blind," Morgan said.

Alec glanced at his brother, trying to hide a flash of panic. Morgan couldn't possibly have guessed that he'd slept with her.

"Mum, she's in her matchmaking mode. I suspect she plans to set me up with Ms. Honeyweather. The woman is rather attractive, I admit. Not my usual type, but she has a nice smile, warm and open. From what mum says, she's quite intelligent, too. I can't imagine why she ever got divorced."

Alec blinked. "You know about that?" How did his brother know but she hadn't said anything to Alec? It was clear she'd told Morgan when they'd only known each other a handful of minutes. She'd spent two nights with Alec and never said a word. That bothered him more than he wanted to admit.

Alec folded his arms over his chest. "I don't think you should seduce mum's ghostwriter."

"Who said anything about seduction?" Morgan pretended to look affronted, but Alec knew better.

"Just leave the woman be."

Morgan grinned. "Hardly seems sporting. If anything, it would disappoint mum. Or perhaps you want in? Best brother wins the girl?"

"If that's the rules, you'll never stand a chance." Alec socked his brother in the arm, just hard enough to make Morgan wince.

"Hey." Morgan started to say something but voices in the hall warned them their mother and Brie were coming back.

"Back so soon?" Morgan took a step toward the two women, but Alec swung his arm out, effectively halting his brother with one dark look.

"Yes, we had a quick cup of tea." Their mother shared a smile with Brie. "Now, you boys can stay or go, but Brie and I must talk Christmas trees."

"We'll stay." Both Alec and Morgan replied at the same time.

Julia walked over to the base of the vast tree with Brie trailing behind her. Brie was still wearing the same cream-colored sweater and jeans she'd worn this morning. Her curves were hinted at but not overly displayed and Alec's hands itched with the sudden need to grip her hips and hold her close so he could press a kiss to her ear. But that was the very last thing he could do right now.

"Martin Luther is the one credited for the tradition of lighting trees," Julia explained to Brie, who scribbled notes in a brightly striped colored notebook. Julia adjusted a few ornaments' positions on the tree as she continued. "The word tinsel is derived from the Latin word *scintilla*, which means spark."

Alec moved closer, drawn in by his mother's history lesson. He'd never realized she knew so much about Christmas.

"They used to use actual shredded silver to make silver leaves as the first tinsel, which must have cost a fortune. Let's see, what else…oh! I'm sure you know that when Queen Victoria married Prince Albert, that's when Christmas trees became popular in England."

"I'd heard that," Brie replied as she wrote down more notes. Alec joined her and Morgan followed too close behind.

"Now, we have a Norway spruce for the salon tree, the same kind Prince Albert chose for Queen Victoria." Julia looked up at the massive tree and Brie did the same. "We can't help but find the tallest one each year.

We like it to be tall enough that the people in the balconies above can almost touch it."

"It's such a lovely tree," Brie said. "My mother used to take me to *The Nutcracker* ballet as a kid and I remember being in awe of the tree on stage. There's a scene where Clara starts to fall asleep and dream of the toy soldier and the mice. During that scene the tree is supposed to grow larger to show that Clara is shrinking to the size of her toys. The ballet company had an actual tree that was made to grow larger from under the stage. You can imagine the effect this had on the kids. I was convinced it was magic how the tree stretched higher and wider while mice peered into the frosted windowpanes." Brie's eyes lit up. He could hear love and affection for the memory so clearly it made his throat tighten.

"I love that ballet too," Julia confessed, then glanced at Alec. "But try convincing my boys to see it? Impossible."

Morgan laughed. "There's no way I would've seen that as a boy, but I would now if someone wished me to." Morgan looked at Brie a little too openly.

"Morgan, why don't you tell Brie about the rope and pulley system we use to get the tree in the place?" Julia suggested.

"I would be happy to." Morgan offered Brie his arm

and then led her around the back of the tree to show her the specially designed tree stand and ropes.

The scene created a pit in Alec's stomach. He had to nip this whole matchmaking thing of his mum's in the bud before Brie got hurt by Morgan's infectious charm.

Alec turned to his mother once Morgan and Brie were out of earshot. "Mum, what are you doing?"

"What do you mean?"

"I mean Morgan..." Alec waved a hand toward his brother. "You know how much of a flirt he is. Just because you want him to find a serious relationship doesn't mean he's going to oblige. Don't do that to Brie."

His mother's eyes narrowed slightly. "I believe they could be good together. Why not give them a chance?"

"Mum, she doesn't want a relationship, all right?"

"You know this how?" Julia arched brow.

"Just trust me. No matchmaking."

"Very well, if you don't want Morgan around her, then I'll need your help with showing Brie around the house."

"If I must..." Alec wanted to fist pump the air in victory, but he acted as if her request was barely tolerable. If his mother wanted him to spend time with Brie, he would. And he would keep his dangerously charming brother far away from her.

7

Brie and Morgan stood by the Christmas tree, but she could see Alec talking with his mother through the decorated branches. It was amazing how similar the two brothers looked now that she was searching for familial resemblances. Both were incredibly sexy, but Morgan had a charming, playful side that was nice to be around. There was something about Alec's reserve mixed with bursts of intensity that drew her in deep, almost drowning her with fascination. Yet, when he let his guard down and teased her with his playful barbs, she couldn't help but respond in kind; it was exciting and fun. But his mercurial nature also confused her. She wasn't quite sure where she stood with him.

Maybe it's because we're both broken. Me with Preston, Alec with his grandfather.

She'd read somewhere that broken people tended to find each other. Seek one another out, often unconsciously. Not that she identified herself as broken, but she still felt the damage after her marriage fell apart. She'd put back all the pieces, like super-gluing a broken vase back together, she knew one good fall might easily fracture it all over again.

The strange thing was that for the longest time she hadn't even known she'd been broken. That first day she'd realized she hadn't missed Preston had been a warning that came far too late. There had been no affairs, no fighting, nothing except a fading away of the life that she'd once believed in so strongly.

And that was how she'd finally understood the depth of her situation. She'd been too weak to fight for anything anymore, too weak to fight for love. Perhaps she wasn't capable of it, or it didn't exist. She honestly didn't know.

"So, what else can I show you?" Morgan asked.

"Actually, it's my turn. I'm taking her to see the Christmas cards." Alec stepped between her and Morgan with an overly polite smile to his brother.

He led her down a wide corridor lined with portraits and busts of solemn looking ancestors made of white marble. A few of the busts had holly wreaths sitting at jaunty angles on their brows. Alec rolled his eyes.

"Morgan's idea."

"He seems like a pranking kind of guy."

Alec suddenly smiled. "You have no idea. He was a nightmare to grow up with."

"Oh yeah? How so?"

"Oh, the usual sibling stuff, I suppose." Alec paused in front of a stern looking Romanesque bust and adjusted the holly wreath, so it sat more evenly upon the statue's head.

"I wouldn't know. I'm an only child." She twirled her pen between her fingers and looked at the bust, rather than at him. In some ways it was easier to talk to the stone face before her. "My dad was quite a few years older than my mom. It was a second marriage for him but a first for her. They had a hard time getting pregnant, so I was the only one they ever had."

Alec put a hand on her shoulder. "I'm sorry," he said. His hazel eyes were full of compassion. It surprised her, but she was relieved as well. She'd wanted to see this side of him. It was something she hadn't seen that often with Preston. Her first husband wasn't lacking in compassion, but he'd never really wanted to talk in depth about personal feelings

"Siblings are often a blessing, but in the case of Morgan, it was most definitely a curse." Alec grinned as he said this, tempering the sting of his words about his brother. "He once put superglue in my shampoo. He stole my Halloween candy almost every year, and he broke a window with a cricket ball and blamed it on me. It was a stained glass one that was two hundred years old. The list goes on, but those are some of his primary offenses."

"And he got away with all of it," she guessed.

Alec tapped the tip of her nose with a fingertip. "Yes. *Every* time."

Brie's heart danced with excitement at this sudden playfulness. It was different than Morgan, she sensed that. When Alec opened himself up, it felt like it wasn't for show. It meant something.

"So, your parents..."

"Both gone," Brie replied. "Dad to a stroke and mom two years later to breast cancer."

"I'm sorry, Brie. I had no idea." Alec stepped closer to her and she remembered they were alone in the hall except for the marble busts. Busts who couldn't judge her as she inched closer to him, not touching, but wishing she could. The hall was open, and anyone could come upon them at any moment. The thought thrilled her, but caution overcame her desire and she drifted back a step to put some distance between them.

"It's fine. It's been years now. I've grieved for them already." But that wasn't completely true. She'd grieved, but there were always days where she felt the pain of their loss almost as fresh as the day they had died. "Why don't you show me the Christmas cards?"

"Right." He escorted her into a beautiful room that had an old-fashioned card table, some bookshelves along one wall, and a grand piano. The piano hosted a dozen Christmas cards propped up on the piano's surface.

"These are from major dignitaries all over the world. And..." He plucked an elegant red and white card and handed it to her. "Including Her Majesty, the Queen."

"The Queen?" Brie accepted the card with reverence.

He held up another. "Queen Máxima of the Netherlands." And another. "And this one is Alois, Hereditary Prince of Liechtenstein." He examined the handwriting of the card. "Though I suspect his wife Sophie is the one who actually wrote it."

"Oh my God, this is amazing." She carefully handed the card back to him.

"Take some pictures if you want."

Brie snapped a dozen photos and when she was done, she saw Alec opening an intricately carved wardrobe off to the side.

"Let me guess. You have a gateway to Narnia too. For your summer home, perhaps?"

Alec laughed. "Not quite. But I did want to show you these." He retrieved a large mahogany box carved with flowers and waved for her to sit next to him on the leather sofa by the card table.

"What is it?"

He cracked open the lid, revealing stacks of cards and letters.

"Merryvale has been receiving cards for almost one hundred and fifty years." He removed one of Christmas cards bound by purple satin ribbons. He slowly flipped through the batch to show her their covers decorated with plump robins on holly branches, wreathes of mistletoe, wintry scenes with children and coachmen with beautiful horses pulling sleighs filled with passengers through the snow.

Alec removed the next batch and treated these with even more care.

"These aren't cards. They're letters from soldiers in the Great War and World War II. Merryvale had many servants and members of the family who fought. My great-grandfather was in the second world war, and his father before him fought in the first."

Alec removed a letter that was tucked into a dusty card that bore an ink sketch of a branch of holly leaves and berries. "This was from my great-great-grandfather. December 12, 1917, postmarked from France."

"Do you mind if I read it?" she asked.

He handed Brie the letter. "Not at all." He relaxed beside her and put an arm around the back of the couch, his fingers brushing the back of her neck briefly as he did so. Brie tried to ignore the electric excitement that his touch created and focused on the letter.

"My dearest Adele,

I wish I could write to you of happy things. Things that would brighten your eyes and win a smile, but here there is only darkness and the creeping fog of war. It chokes the lives out of the men around me. Many of us sleep upright in the trenches, our hands clasping photos of our wives and sweethearts. I don't know which is worse, the shells or the yellow gas that drifts into our holes.

I hate that I'm even writing to you of such things. I fear though if I do not write them down, they will be trapped inside me forever. I miss you and I miss Merryvale. The snow here is gray, from the ash of distant fires.

I hope that when you think of me, you will keep me with you in your heart so that I may be there beside you for

Christmas. I long for Cook's pudding, the caroling, the hot wassail drinks, and the sight of a tall spruce tree in the salon glinting with tinsel. I wish I could see the blanket of pure white on the grounds and the hounds bounding through it.

That is my Christmas wish. To come home to you.

Yours always,

Robert."

Brie stared at the yellowed letter with the words scrawled in faded ink, more brown now than black.

"What happened to them?" She turned to see Alec was staring into the distance, his gaze unfocused.

"Robert never made it home. An officer who served with him wrote Adele a letter telling her how he'd gone over the top a few days after that letter was written. He died trying to save his fellow soldiers who were trapped in barbed wire. The Germans had left them alive to lure others to their rescue. He didn't know it was a trap until it was too late." Alec finally looked at her, his gaze completely focused. "His son was born a few months later. He never even knew Adele had been pregnant with their child."

"The way he spoke of Christmas here at Merryvale, the natural magic of it, and his hopes and dreams was beautiful. I would like to include that in the book, if your mother agrees." Brie wanted to clutch the heart-breaking letter to her chest but instead she carefully folded it back up and returned the letter inside the card.

"He was an artist," Alec mused. "I imagine he drew this because there were no cards on the front line." He brushed his thumb over the ink sketch of the holly leaves, the detail seemed even more powerful once Brie knew where it had come from.

"Why don't we talk like that anymore?" she asked Alec as she carefully put the cards back into the box.

"Like what?"

"Like the world is beautiful, like nature and other people still matter. Everyone I know is obsessed with social media, with the latest app on their phones, or with reality TV. And then you think of people like Robert who were dying a world away from their home and the only thing that mattered to them was the people and places they loved. It breaks my heart."

Brie couldn't bring herself to say it, but that was what she dreamed of when she'd married Preston: a life full of a love that would defy the ages. She wanted to be loved like that, but it had only been an illusion. Maybe that was why she couldn't trust herself to love, because the type of love she believed in didn't exist anymore.

But it had. The proof was right here.

Alec gripped her shoulder as he simply held her against his side for a long moment.

"This is why I hate coming home," he finally said. "The older I get the more painful I find it here. More loss and death."

"But that's life, isn't it?" Brie found a small smile somewhere within her. "The highs of life mean nothing without the lows."

Alec didn't reply but he didn't pull away either. There was a gentle comfort of being together in this moment, like last night while the snowstorm raged outside.

"Alec...we shouldn't tell anyone what happened last night," Brie finally said. "We can't..." She struggled for words. "We can't do that again and we can't let anyone know what happened. I could get fired from my publisher."

"I agree," Alec said just as quietly. "No one can know about last night. We'll keep things professional." He dropped his arms from her shoulders and she instantly missed his warmth.

She opened her mouth to speak when she heard some shouts from the main hall.

"We better go see what that is." Alec led the way. Outside the room, they found Thad, Veronica, and their daughter Lyra covered with snow in the doorway. They were shrugging out of their heavy coats, hats, and mittens. Their faces were deep pink from the cold outside.

"Brie!" Veronica rushed over and hugged her. She didn't miss the happy glow in her friend's face. Marriage to Thad had been so good for her.

"What have you guys been up to?" Brie asked as Thad removed a large blue striped scarf off of Lyra in such a way that Lyra twirled like a cartoon mummy being unwrapped. It filled Brie's heart with joy to see them laugh like this. She still couldn't believe how easily Thad had taken to fatherhood. But given how sweet Lyra was, it was no surprise. It was impossible not to love the little girl.

Veronica laughed as she removed her woolen cap and gloves. "We've been sledding. You have to try it. They have sleds large enough for adults and really big hills. It was so much fun. I haven't done that since I was a kid." A servant collected the winter clothes and put them into the coat closet.

"Are Thad's parents coming over for the holidays too?"

"No, not this year. They wanted to give us some time with Lyra, just the three of us." Veronica pulled her aside as more people came into the entryway. "Now, I know you were on the plane that had that emergency landing, so be honest with me. Are you okay?" The nurse in Veronica was out in full force, wanting to protect and fix anything she could.

"I'm okay. It was bad last night, but Alec was there. We sort of stuck together during the whole thing. He was quite brave and kept me safe."

"Alec was?" Veronica leaned over to look at Alec, who was across the room chatting with Thad and Lyra. "*That* Alec?"

"Yeah, he was amazing. We were getting ready to do the emergency landing and he put his arm around me. He shielded me. He was..." Honestly she did know what to say, except it was truly brave.

"You've met Morgan, right?" Veronica steered her focus toward the younger brother, who had just joined the group along with Byron.

"Yes, I met him. He's nice. Funny." She watched Lyra pretend to punch Morgan who then doubled over and pretended to die on the carpet.

"Men will always still be boys at heart." Veronica laughed. "Morgan is so good with Lyra."

"He is." Brie agreed, but her gaze strayed to Alec who was standing beside Thad. He threw some suggestions to Lyra about how best to wrestle with Morgan. Brie swore she heard him tell Lyra to punch his brother in the kidneys.

"Everyone is finally here!" Julia was beaming as she

joined Brie and Veronica. Morgan had been right; the countess did have boundless energy that not only fueled her excitement but made her light up with a pure, contagious joy.

"I was thinking we could all make Christmas cookies this afternoon. I want Brie to see the kitchens and try out a few of our traditional recipes. And Mrs. Fitzhugh is most excited to show off her culinary expertise for the book. Does that sound like a good idea?" Julia asked Brie.

"That sounds great."

"I'm sure Lyra will do anything if it involves cookies," Veronica chuckled.

"Wonderful." Julia turned toward the group of men. "Cookies in the kitchens!"

Lyra climbed off a panting but laughing Morgan. "Cookies?"

"Cookies?" Alec held out a hand to his brother and helped him up, then came toward Brie and Veronica.

"Yep, we're going to decorate them. Care to show me your skills, Mr. Investment Banker?" Brie challenged.

Alec's smirked and leaned close to her ear. "I give great cookie, so watch out." He then followed the rest of the family into the kitchens.

"What the heck was that?" Veronica demanded.

Brie stared at her friend. "What?"

"*I give good cookie?*" Veronica quoted. "If I didn't know Alec better, I would say he was trying to flirt with you. He needs practice."

"He wasn't flirting with me," Brie argued. "We bonded a little because of the whole crash thing and I felt like teasing him about his fancy stressful job. It's kind of our thing."

"But you admit you have a thing."

"Not *that* kind of thing," Brie sighed. "And stop trying to set me up with Morgan. I could see that coming a mile away."

"I wasn't...okay I *was*. But you would be so cute together." Veronica almost whined. "Please let me set you up. *Please?*"

"No, absolutely not." The last thing she needed was her best friend playing Cupid.

"You're no fun," Veronica pretended to pout. "Everyone spent so long trying to set me up with men. Now I want the chance."

"Let me open up a cook coffee house and start an open mic night. Then maybe I can find the love of my life singing his heart out to me." Brie nudged Veronica with an elbow and they both giggled.

"You joke, but it worked out well for me." Veronica grinned as she watched Thad ahead of them. Veronica had been trying to support herself and her young daughter after losing her husband when she'd been pregnant and that coffee shop had been the way she'd been able to afford the brownstone house in Chicago that her father had given to her before he died. Thad had come in one night during an open mic night to sing and it had pretty much love at first sight. Not that things had been easy for them at first, but it had all worked out in the end.

When Brie and Veronica entered the huge kitchens in Merryvale Court, Brie gasped. A trio of cooks were hard at work on one long roughhewn wood table. The cooks smiled at them and returned to their preparations. A second long counter opposite them was covered with gingerbread house materials and cookie prep stations.

Alec, Morgan, Lyra, Thad, and Byron were huddled together at the gingerbread supply area, talking excitedly about what they planned to build. Julia watched them with a wide grin on her face. Brie sidled up beside her.

"Looks like that will keep them busy."

"It certainly will." Julia laughed. "They have enough gingerbread there to build a village. I thought we could start on the cookies. But first, I want to show you what the cooks are working on, our famous Christmas cake."

Brie waved to Veronica, who had joined Thad and Lyra for a moment. Then she got her pen and notebook out as Julia took her to the long table where a beautiful round cake sat on a plate.

"We don't know exactly when we started making these here in England, but they are a lot like the infamous British Christmas pudding we serve. We make them a few weeks in advance, and you need to keep it moist with a regular supply of brandy."

"How do you do that?" The cake was covered in white marzipan frosting and topped with three cedar trees sculpted from icing. One of the cooks had taken a fat red ribbon and wound it around the base, then covered it with a gauzy slender gold ribbon over the top of the red ribbon. Then the cake had been artfully laid on a plate next to a few cinnamon sticks bound with red plaid ribbon. A trio of small pinecones with gold dusted over the top sat on the other side of the cake, resting on the plate. The effect was stunning.

The countess nodded at a second cake not yet covered with icing. "You pierce the bottom with a skewer and carefully pour three or four tablespoons of brandy, and you repeat this every four or five days. It's a complex recipe, but at least you can see the finished cake."

She collected a slip of paper from one of the cooks

showed it to Brie, who snapped a photo of the ingredients and cooking directions. Brie thanked the cooks and then went to the Christmas cookie station.

"Every year I bake two hundred cookies, which I usually decorate with Byron and Morgan's help. We deliver the cookies to the Children's Hospital half an hour from here. Something to give the children some extra cheer."

"Alec doesn't help?"

Julia shook her head. "He usually isn't home for Christmas. I can't tell you how rare it is that he's here at all. Thad and Veronica worked a miracle to get him to come." Her eyes softened as she watched Alec and Morgan start building their houses.

Julia gave her an encouraging nudge toward the workstation were Morgan and Alec were setting up. "I believe I can handle the cookies. Why don't you go help them?" Brie knew better than to argue with the matriarch of an English household, especially one with this much energy.

Brie went to the gingerbread station and nudged Alec's arm with hers. "Need help?"

He smirked as he subtly moved between her and Morgan. "No, but you can tell me what you think of my castle." He pointed at the lopsided tower of gingerbread.

"Yeah, you need help." Brie grinned cheekily at him. "I sure hope you're a better investment banker than you are a gingerbread architect." Brie adjusted the walls of his tower, then carefully applied more icing to the wall before holding it in place to let the icing set. Alec placed his hands over hers, both of them holding the pieces together. His warm hands engulfed her own. The simple connection of their palms felt comforting, though a bit dangerous and forbidden.

Morgan shot them an appraising look. "Cheating, already? You can't bring in a ringer, Alec." Morgan complained but when Brie glanced over at him, he winked at her. "I believe that's what you Americans call it."

"You never mentioned that in the rules," Alec countered, the light of a challenge in his eyes.

Brie shook her head, but she didn't stop helping Alec construct a wall for his castle. She'd made a couple of gingerbread houses in her day, and while she was no master, she could hold her own. Beside them, Morgan was surreptitiously stealing glances so he could mimic her technique.

"Pass the gumdrops?" Brie asked Alec.

Alec handed her the bowl and their fingers brushed. A spark shot between them as their gaze briefly met then separated.

"So...did you get all your work done yesterday?" she asked Alec casually as they worked.

"I did, but I've already been assigned a new project that I'll be spearheading over Christmas. An acquisition."

Morgan's eyes brightened with interest. "Oh? What firm will you engage?"

Alec swept a knife with frosting down the side of the stirrer, frowning at the messiness of it. "Not sure just yet who the client will choose."

"I know a few excellent solicitors who would be happy to handle it." Morgan was focused on his own gingerbread house again.

"Thanks. I'll be sure to let them know."

Brie's attention shot back and forth between the two brothers, a little amused, but mostly fascinated. They were both involved in hard, demanding careers, yet here they were decorating gingerbread castles in a country house that was over four centuries old. It was just another day for them. For her, it was a fantasy come to life. She'd grown up on Long Island in the shadows of the *Great Gatsby* era oil mansions. But those homes had been closed to her, as unapproachable as Mount Olympus in the clouds.

By the time the cookies were done baking, the group helped Julia bundle them into little care packages made of red cellophane and tucked them into a large basket.

"Does anyone want to come with me to the hospital?" Julia asked.

"Morgan and I need to set up a few of the smaller Christmas trees along the driveway," Byron announced. Julia left the kitchen to have the car pulled around.

"I'd like to go with you," Brie volunteered.

"I'll go as well," Alec added. Brie glanced at him and he shrugged.

"If I don't steer clear of him, Morgan might try to drop a Christmas tree on me." She was glad he was going with her. She'd decided to make it her mission to convince Alec to get back into the spirit of Christmas. Reconnect with his family. Julia had given her such a wonderful gift, and Brie wanted to return the favor.

Veronica met Brie's eyes from across the room and mouthed. *"O. M. G. He's going with you!"*

Brie shook her head at Veronica, who winked at her.

"Why don't we get our coats?" Alec put his hand on the small of her back and ushered her out into the hall.

When they were alone, Brie gasped as he pulled her into an alcove between two paintings and claimed her mouth with his. The kiss was quick, possessive and intense, and left her feeling a little dazed. When he pulled away, enough to let her breathe at least, she blinked up at him.

"What was that for?" she whispered. "I thought we agreed. Professional, remember?"

Alec brushed her thumb over her lips and smirked in that way that made her womb clench in excitement. "That was professional. My most professional kiss. I just wanted to give you a reason not to think about my brother."

"Think about Morgan? But I□"

He silenced her with another softer kiss that left her heart hammering in her chest. His dark brown lashes lowered and his eyes, with that warm hazel green, shimmered in the gilded lamplight above them.

"Alec, we can't do this." Yet even as she protested, her mind was filled with a dozen erotic thoughts of them slipping into each other's beds and their bodies sliding skin to skin beneath the covers. Maybe no one would find out...

"I've been thinking about that," he murmured in that irresistible British accent. "It's only one week. We can do this. Have a casual fling, right? No one would have to know and when we leave, we'd go back to our lives..."

"We'd be done." Brie finished for him. It was the most tempting offer she'd had in a long time.

His eyes swept over her face and down her body in an almost tangible caress that left her humming with desire. "Think it over." He left to fetch their coats.

With her heart pounding, she followed him. What was she going to do? Say yes? Risk her book deal with his mother? Risk her job? But how did she say no to someone whose very touch set her on fire?

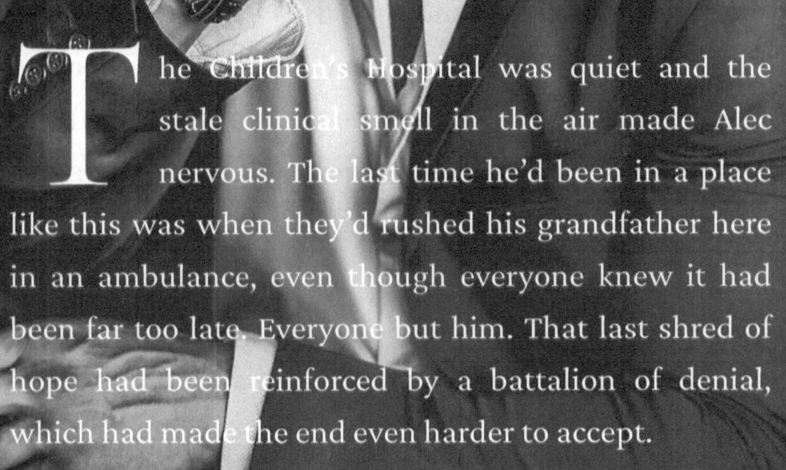

8

The Children's Hospital was quiet and the stale clinical smell in the air made Alec nervous. The last time he'd been in a place like this was when they'd rushed his grandfather here in an ambulance, even though everyone knew it had been far too late. Everyone but him. That last shred of hope had been reinforced by a battalion of denial, which had made the end even harder to accept.

Someone had hung some Christmas decorations in the wing to try to make things cheerier, but there was very little that they could do to make the children feel better.

Alec's mother and Brie walked ahead of him, while he carried a large wicker basket full of brightly colored packages of homemade frosted cookies.

His mother met the charge nurse at the nurse's station and obtained a list of rooms of all the patients staying in the children's oncology wing who'd had parents agree to allow this special visit ahead of time and signed waivers allowing visitors.

"There are twelve children we can visit that aren't in the ICU. The nurse thought that getting some treats will cheer them up," Julia said. Her throat caught as she looked at Brie and Alec. He knew how much this hurt her, yet she put herself through it every year.

"If you'd like, I'll handle the list." Brie took the paper from his mother and collected a package of cookies. "Luke Atkins, age fourteen." She walked to the first room and knocked on the door. Someone told her to come in and she entered, Alec and Julia following behind.

Luke sat in his hospital bed, a handheld video game in his hands.

"Hi Luke, my name is Brie. This is Alec and Julia." Brie gestured in their direction. "I hope you don't mind us visiting. We made some cookies if you'd like some."

Luke looked both embarrassed and excited, but after a moment the boy relaxed and set the videogame aside.

He accepted the package Brie handed him. "I like cookies. What kind are they?"

"Sugar cookies. You'll be bouncing off the ceiling all night," Brie teased. His face split into a grin

"That would be pretty funny." Luke tested one of the cookies with a tentative bite and Brie pointed at his game.

"What are you playing?"

"Nighthawk. It's a spy game set in ancient times."

"How ancient?" Brie asked.

"The 1980s."

"Okay, now I want to smack him," muttered Alec, but only loud enough for Brie and Julia to hear.

"Cool, sounds like fun," Brie said to drown him out. They talked for another ten minutes before Alec and Julia helped pass out the rest of the cookies to the other patients.

At first, it wasn't easy for Alec to hand out cookies to the children. But the more time he spent around them, talked with them, tried to cheer them up, the more he realized that it felt good to be here. Soon, he was teasing the children and getting them to laugh while they ate their sugary treats.

Brie caught up to him while he was making his last stop to a girl named Trina, aged eight, according to the list. Trina was a tiny thing with big blue eyes, but her features were gaunt and her skin a worrisome gray color. Her mother was sitting in a chair at the girl's bedside reading a book to her.

"Hi," Alec said quietly when Trina's mother looked up from the bed. "We have some Christmas cookies for her if she would like some." Alec held out the red cellophane wrapped package.

"Thank you. She would love them," the mother said. Her face was bright with a cheery smile, but Alec could see the worry and weariness behind it. He couldn't imagine having to care for a child with cancer. To watch a young life go through so much pain, and possibly death...it was unbearable.

Brie sat with the girl and asked if she could finish reading the book.

"Thanks, I could actually use a minute," the mom admitted. She stepped into the hall and Julia went with her, putting an arm around the woman's shoulders. Alec was certain Julia would know what to do to help the exhausted woman. He certainly didn't.

Alec sat down beside Brie in the second chair and watched her read to Trina. The girl listened with rapt attention. It wasn't a child's book; it was a novel called *The Last Unicorn* by Peter S. Beagle.

"You know, this was my favorite book as a child," Brie told Trina.

"It was?" The girl's voice was melodic like a songbird.

"Yes, you've read it before?"

The girl grinned. "Yep! My mom even let me see the movie. It was a cartoon, but it's still good." Trina opened her cookie parcel and took out a tree-shaped snack.

"Would you like me to read a little?" Brie opened the book where the bookmark rested.

"Yes please." Trina leaned forward, her small delicate body still managing to carry some excitement despite her illness. She adjusted the stocking cap covering her bald scalp.

Brave, beautiful child, Alec thought.

Brie began to read aloud. Just as Alec had thought that first time he met her, she *should* narrate books. She used accents and special voices with ease, making the little girl laugh. By the time Trina had eaten half her cookies, she looked relaxed and fresh color blossomed faintly in her pale face.

Trina's mother returned with a grateful look and reclaimed her seat. Brie and Alec said goodbye to the little girl.

"I'll check out with the nurses and call for the car," Julia said, leaving them for a moment in the hospital hallway. Alec held the mostly empty basket and turned to Brie. Her face was drawn and she was quiet. He wondered what was wrong, but quickly remembered that Brie had lost her mother to cancer. This had to be bringing back hard memories for her.

"You okay?" he asked.

She tried to smile but the expression floundered. "No...not really. Those poor kids. I'm trying so hard not to think about how much they're suffering because it can drown a person but spending the afternoon here...it was good and a bit awful at the same time." She sighed.

"That doesn't make sense, does it?" Alec gently caught her chin and lifted her face.

"Hey. I know *exactly* what you mean. No one likes to feel useless, and that's exactly how we feel. We cannot slay their dragons, but we can give them a few hours of smiles and a dangerous amount of sugar." He smiled at her, feeling a cottony warmth in his chest.

She smiled back. "Slay their dragons... I like that."

"My grandfather used to say it. Sometimes you want to help someone but the only thing you can do is spend time with them. He used to say, '*Alec my boy, you cannot slay another man's dragons, but you can be that man's friend.*'"

Brie's eyes softened with understanding as she gazed up at him. "I would have liked your grandfather."

"He would have loved you." Alec stroked his thumb

over her cheek, tracing the faint smile lines around her mouth. Her sweetness was killing him.

"We should go before your mother sends a search party," Brie said, stepping back.

Alec waited in the hall a few seconds before going after her. He'd meant what he'd said before. He'd *wanted* to be with her again. He wanted however many nights he could steal with her while she stayed at Merryvale. He knew she wanted him, too. He'd tasted the way she'd responded to his kiss, but she was holding back. He would have to show her that a hidden passion might just be what they both needed.

BRIE HAD DINNER WITH ALEC'S FAMILY, PLUS THAD AND Veronica. The formal dining room was put to good use. The dogs waited, half-hidden beneath the white table-cloth, as the first course was carried in. Copper and Pepper were silent except for the sounds of their tails thumping on the ground. Yogi must have been some-where nearby because they could hear his heavy breathing, and Lyra kept covering her mouth to hide her laughter at whatever the bulldog was doing below the table.

Wedged between Alec and Morgan, Brie was once

again treated to the humor of the brothers playfully antagonizing one another as everyone enjoyed their white onion and truffle soup.

"Fetch your notebook," Alec said to her in a husky whisper. "I can tell you this recipe."

Brie pulled her notebook from her bag and scribbled the ingredients and cooking instructions down.

"How do you know this one?" she asked.

"One should always memorize their favorite dish by heart."

"Actually, it's the only one he knows." Morgan leaned in to whisper from other the other side. "Alec could burn a pot of hot water."

Alec shot a glare at Morgan. "You don't know how to cook either."

"Not true." Morgan shot back. "I know how to make Christmas pudding."

"Only the part that requires the brandy." Alec leaned back in his chair smugly. "And that's because you drink most of it."

"Uh, guys?" Brie whispered.

"What?" they asked in unison.

"Everyone is staring," Brie tucked her notebook under her chair and took a spoonful of the creamy pale soup, trying to ignore everyone else at the table.

"Would anyone like some sloe gin?" Byron asked after he shot his misbehaving sons an intense look.

"I would love a glass," Thad replied before he winked at Brie from further down the table.

Relieved at the distraction, she was able to write more notes about the dark gin made from sloes. Byron explained that sloes were the fruit of Blackthorn plants which grew wild on the Merryvale property.

After a dinner of mince pies and beetroot chutney, the group retired to the salon to watch the countess light the tree. The main lights above them on the walls were dimmed and everyone counted down to one before Julia plugged in the cord. Brie held her breath in awe as sparkling, brilliant light illuminated the room.

"Beautiful, isn't it?" Alec asked from behind her.

His hand touched the space between her shoulder blades, sending a shiver through her as he moved his hand down her body. "Yes."

She was an instrument he was bringing to life right here in this room. The more he touched her, the more she wanted to make music. His offer of a secret tryst for just a week, just the two of them bound by passion, could she do it? They would simply be exercising their desires in a healthy way. It didn't have to be about commitment. What was wrong with that?

She reached one hand behind her and he slipped his hand into hers. "Alec."

"Yes?" He stepped closer, hiding the connection of their hands.

"Come to me tonight."

He squeezed her hand to indicate he'd heard her, then let go and stepped carefully away. She joined Thad and Veronica, who were watching Lyra examine the tree.

"So...how was the hospital?" Thad asked her. "I've been there a few times. It's a wonderful facility, but it's difficult to see those children hurting."

"Yes, it was hard but very much worth it." Brie hadn't been prepared for the pain at seeing those young lives and the lives of their families suffering. Yet she'd known it was important to visit and to give those kids a few minutes where they felt normal. She'd been amazed at how Alec had spoken with the children. He was quiet at first, but seemed so at ease with them by the end. She expected him to freeze up or be unable to relate, but the exact opposite had happened.

"So, what's happening tomorrow?" Lyra asked as she joined them.

"More sledding? And visiting a Christmas fair in the village nearby, I think." Thad looked at Veronica for confirmation and she nodded.

"Tomorrow is Christmas Eve," Lyra reminded him.

"It certainly is." Veronica laughed. "I hope Santa will find his way here for your presents."

Lyra looked at her mother with hope in her eyes. "I hope he does too." She left to pet the dogs who'd just come running into the room.

"Thank god she still believes in Santa Claus," Veronica mused. "I hate that she's growing up so fast."

Thad put an arm around Veronica's waist and leaned in to kiss her temple. "That's why we should talk about having a baby. Lyra needs a sibling."

Veronica kissed Thad's cheek. "Oh, is *that* why? I thought you just like the practice of making babies?"

"I love nothing more than *practicing* with you." With a smirk, Thad let her go and walked over to join Lyra and the dogs.

"You're so lucky," Brie said.

Veronica's brows drew together. "Lucky?"

"Yeah, things with you and Thad *work*. You care about each other. It's not just physical."

Veronica seemed to understand what Brie was too afraid to say. "Brie, what happened with Preston wasn't your fault. People who marry young don't always know the difference between infatuation and affection."

"Trust me. I know that now." She looked down at

her feet, her face a little flushed. "I'm just worried I'll never be able to tell, you know?"

Her friend gave her a hug. "Just open yourself up. The universe will make something happen."

Brie wanted to believe Veronica but couldn't. She was too afraid to give her love life a second chance, She didn't want to deny herself the chance to be with Alec. Maybe if she just embraced a relationship that was strictly a matter of lust and attraction, she wouldn't be disappointed. Sex with him had been explosive, powerful, and intimate in a way that made her hungry for more.

Alec slipped away from the group while everyone enjoyed hot toddies or hot chocolate. He wandered the halls of the old manor house until he stopped at his grandfather's study. Although he'd obviously been drawn to it like a magnet, he hadn't even realized he was walking in this direction. His hand shook as he touched the door latch, but with a deep breath, he opened it. Memories assailed him as he stared about the room.

Nothing had changed. Two tall African spears stood in one corner, whispering tales of when Walter had been a young man. He hadn't hunted on safari like many of his peers. Instead, he'd helped a chief in Kenya hunt down a group of poachers to save a herd of elephants. The chief had given him this pair of warrior spears as a gift.

Alec ran his finger over the head of the nearest spear. The cold metal was smooth and sharpened to a deadly point. Thin, rough rope bound the dark wood of the shaft to the spearhead.

Behind the spears was an old black-and-white photo of his grandfather with his arm around a young chief's shoulder. Walter couldn't have been much older than Alec in that photo.

How many stories had been lost when his grandfather had died? The whole room was a powerful shrine to Walter's life. War medals were carefully displayed in a case on the desk. Alec remembered wanting to wear them when he played soldier with Morgan. Byron had never wanted to let them, but Walter had chuckled and pinned the medal to Alec's chest.

"It's just a bit of metal and ribbon," Walter had told Byron. "The men who fought beside me wouldn't mind, not if it gives the boys a sense of honor while they play."

Alec remembered how carefully he'd played while wearing the war medal, knowing only a little of the sacrifices his grandfather had made to earn such an honor. He'd been a young man when he'd fought in Korea and had lost several friends.

War is not pretty. It's not something a man wishes for, but peace can't always be earned by kindness. Sometimes evil can only be stopped when good men go to war. Walter's voice seemed to echo in the room from a lifetime ago.

Alec opened the box of medals and ran his finger along the collection: the Victorian Cross, the Military Cross, the George Medal, and the Queen's Gallantry Medal. The silver on the medals was still shining even after all these years.

Beside the box of medals was a leather-bound journal with his grandfather's initials and a date in the 1960s. A leather strap bound the journal tight, protecting whatever thoughts Walter had jotted down. As much as Alec wanted to read it, it was too much like peering into his grandfather's soul. Far too private a thing for him to open uninvited.

"I haven't had the heart to change anything," his father said behind him. Alec turned to see Byron leaning against the door jamb, arms crossed over his chest.

"I'm glad you didn't." Alec's gaze swept over the bookshelves that lined one wall. There were artifacts from all over the world tucked in between books almost as an afterthought. "It's like he's still here."

"In a way, he is." Byron moved deeper into the room beside Alec. "He was an amazing man. I wish you could have had more time with him." Byron picked up the leather journal and held it out to Alec. "He wrote hundreds of these over the course of his life. You should read one."

"What? No, I can't—"

His father pressed the journal against Alec's chest. "I insist. Discover who he really was. I know that his death still affects you in ways it never has with Morgan. We all handle death differently. But you should know him, *the real him*. He would want you to."

Alec's hands curled around the leather which had grown soft with age. "Have you read it?"

His father nodded. "I read everything of his about two months after he died. It brought me closer to him. I think you need that, Alec." His father patted his shoulder and left Alec alone again in his grandfather's study.

With the journal clutched in one hand, Alec looked around the study once more. The large walnut wood desk had always had a drawer of peppermint hard candies and the pocket watch now resting on the black leather desk protector had never left his father's side.

Alec picked up his grandfather's watch and pressed down on the knob to make the lid pop open. The black hands were stopped. Alec twisted the top of the watch, cranking the knob back, feeling the little gears work as the watch wound up. When he pressed the knob down again, the hands began to move. He adjusted the time and set the watch back on the desk, face open.

He left the study and went to his bedchamber where he poured himself a glass of brandy before he settled in a chair by the fire. Perhaps his father was right. Perhaps it was time to really get to know the man he'd loved fiercely and lost.

9

Brie changed into her black and pink short-sleeved button up shirt and short pajama set, brushed her teeth, and washed her face in the expensive Italian marble bathroom connected to her room. It felt like she was spending a night in an honest-to-God princess suite.

Whoever said fairytales weren't real had never stayed in Merryvale. Her walls were covered with floor-to-ceiling tapestries of deer walking through the English woods. In the corner of one hanging, there was a darker area of the woods that held a wolf, half hidden in a set of bushes. The wolf gave the tapestry an edge of menace that intrigued her. No doubt there was some story behind it. She would have to ask the countess about it later.

Brie climbed onto the tall four poster bed and pulled her coat toward her. She dug into the pockets and found the business card Alec had given her. His name, along with the last name that would have given away his relation to her client if only she'd taken the time to look, was printed in a neat block letter font. Beneath it was the Barclays logo as well as the address of his investment banking division in London. Alec's office phone and mobile number were near the bottom.

She brushed her thumb over the number and then tapped it into her phone and saved it to her contacts. After a brief moment of hesitation, she typed out a text.

Brie: I'm in bed. Waiting for you.

She paused before she hit send. Was that too on the nose? She didn't want to come off too forward. She erased the message and typed another.

Brie: You Up? ;-)

Then she muttered as she deleted that message as well. She was twenty-nine, too old to send a winking face emoji to a man she was hoping would get naked with her very soon. She wasn't a teenager.

Brie: I meant what I said by the tree.

Perfect. Not too aggressive, not too teenage-y. Just the truth. She hit send and held her breath. A moment later three dots appeared as Alec started to reply.

Alec: You found my business card?

Brie: Yes.

Alec: Good. I was worried you asked my mum for my number.

Brie bit her lip to keep from laughing.

Brie: I don't think it would've been good to ask her for your number. God knows how she would react if she knew why I wanted it.

Alec: She'd either faint or throw a parade. Best to keep this our little secret.

Brie: Agreed. So...

She didn't want to outright invite him over.

Alec: Which room are you in?

Brie: Uh, I don't know. The one with the forest tapestry that has a scary wolf half hidden in one corner.

Alec: The forest room. Be there shortly.

She giggled at that.

Brie: The forest room? That's unoriginal.

Alec: This house has over fifty bedrooms. You run out of clever names after a while.

Brie slid off the bed and tucked her phone back into her purse. Her heart hammered and her blood beat a steady rhythm in her ears as she started to second-guess what she was doing. Maybe this wasn't such a good idea.

She jumped at the soft knock at her door. When she

opened it, Alec was there in his jeans and sweater, holding a bottle of scotch and two glasses. Tucked under one arm was a leather journal. Brie let him slide past her into her room and shut the door.

"I thought you might be a little nervous and liquid courage can help." His gaze drifted down her body to her bare feet and legs, and his lips curved in a crooked grin that made her flush.

"The drink would be great," she admitted. Trying to have a casual, sexy fling was new to her and she was anxious. A little liquid courage was definitely in order.

Alec set the glasses down on one of the nightstands and placed the leather journal next to it before he poured the scotch into them.

"Single malt whiskey," he said as he handed her a glass. She took a sip. It burned, nearly choking her and she coughed in response. He patted her back as she recovered.

"The second sip goes down smoother," he assured her.

He was right. The next sip went down smoothly. It still burned, but in a different way. Her body started to hum with the heat from the whiskey.

"So..." She pointed at the wolf. "What's the story behind that?"

There had to be hundreds of mysteries in this old

home, hidden in the paintings, dusty black and white photos nestled in old frames, artifacts that might be centuries old. She wanted to know the stories behind them all.

Alec sipped his whiskey and walked over to examine the wolf in the tapestry. "Don't tell Morgan I told you, but this tapestry used to give him nightmares. He was terrified of the wolf. He said that it used to come out of the fabric in his dreams. He would see these red eyes…" Alec reached out and touched the eyes, which she noticed did have some red thread mixed in with the black that made the beast's eyes glow.

"That would have given me nightmares too." The more she stared at it the scarier it became. "It still might."

Alec chuckled. "I'll be here to protect you." He winked at her and for a second he seemed more like his playful younger brother. "Let's see, what do I remember…?" He faced the wolf tapestry again. "My family received this tapestry from the noble Wolfe family. One of our ancestors in the eighteenth century married into the Wolfe family and became Viscountess Wolfe. The gift she sent home to us was this tapestry. It's said that so long as Merryvale possesses it, the house is protected by the wolf's magic."

"Magic?" Brie almost laughed but stopped herself when she saw Alec was completely serious.

"What kind of magic, we don't know. But for everything that dies within these walls, the lands grow something else," Alec's voice softened as he tilted his head. "The day after my grandfather died, the cherry trees blossomed. They had been dormant during the winter, but they exploded into bloom. A hundred trees all at once on Boxing Day, just after a heavy snowfall, and they stayed in bloom the rest of the winter. Every arborist nearby was astounded and none could explain it."

"Magic," Brie echoed in wondrous understanding. Sometimes things happened in life that didn't seem possible, yet they happened anyway. "So, this wolf protects Merryvale?"

"According to the legends, he does it in honor of our ancestor who left the home she loved to marry a stranger. You see, my ancestor didn't love Viscount Wolfe, nor he her, the marriage was one of necessity. But they came to love each other most passionately."

"Do you think I could write about that story in the book?"

Alec was quiet for a long moment. "I suppose. But why? I thought it was a Christmas traditions book."

"It is, but I want to share the beauty of this place,

the stories, the magic, it all matters. It's all part of Merryvale."

"For book sales, naturally." His words held a slight bite as he finished his scotch.

"No," she shook her head fiercely. "That doesn't matter to me. It never has." How could she explain to him the power of words, the power of stories? "I don't write for money. I write because stories matter. Tales of human experience *matter*."

Alec's sighed and turned to face her. "I'm sorry. I'm not used to sharing things about Merryvale. Ever since they started filming that blasted Regency miniseries here, my parents have been dealing with overeager fans and other madness."

"I get it. You're a bit protective. There's nothing wrong with that." She put a hand on his arm, and he tapped her glass.

"Finish your drink."

"Why?" She raised a brow, smiling. "You want to get me drunk?"

"No!" He chuckled. "I want you to drink it because that scotch is bloody expensive, and I'd hate to waste it."

"Oh." She tipped the glass back and finished it, letting the burn of warm her whole body up.

"But also because I want you relaxed." He cupped

her chin, gazing into her eyes in a way that made her dizzier than the alcohol ever could.

"Just for the record, I haven't really done this before." She couldn't look away as he took a step closer to her.

"Done what?" Alec brushed the pad of his thumb over her bottom lip.

"Had a casual hookup."

"I've had a few in my day." His admission filled her with mix of jealousy and curiosity.

"Okay, so how do we do this? You'll have to walk me through it." She was almost rambling now, but God, she was nervous. They had already slept together but this was different. She had no plane crash adrenaline to deal with now and they were going into this situation with their eyes wide open, not like their first spontaneous hook up.

Alec leaned in. "We do it however you like," he whispered just before he kissed her. His lips explored her mouth. "We can take all night, or we can do it hard and fast...maybe even both. Whatever you desire."

"Slow is good." Brie closed her eyes as he kissed her again. He wove his fingers through her hair and sighed as though it gave him pleasure. Alec's mouth on hers told her how much he wanted her. She remembered how good it felt to be *wanted*, to be desired. He broke the kiss to nibble playfully at her bottom lip.

"I want to strip you naked and fuck you on the bed," he said in a low and deliciously dark tone.

Brie trembled as she reached for the buttons of her top. "Okay..."

"Allow me." He took his time, his fingers slowly sliding the buttons through the slits. When he finished, he parted her nightshirt and his hands curled in the fabric of her collar. He gazed down at her exposed breasts.

"Christ, you're perfect." He peeled the shirt off her and let it drop to the ground before he cupped one breast, filling his palm and rolling the nipple with this thumb. The passion she'd attributed to the adrenaline from the crash the previous night was still there. In fact, it was stronger than ever. Alec's lips curved in an indulgent smile as he slid one hand between the waistband of her shorts and panties to cup her mound.

"Oh, God." She clutched his shoulders when he slid a finger inside her.

"I've had so many fantasies of doing this to you, darling," he said as he leaned in to kiss her neck.

"Me too," Brie was dazed with arousal and couldn't resist teasing him. "I've had fantasies...like on the plane."

"What kind?" Alec's lips whispered against her skin.

"Before the crash I dreamed you bent me over in the airplane bathroom and touched me like you did just now."

He groaned and his hand down her shorts stilled for a moment. "You're going to bloody kill me, you know that?"

"Want to act it out?" Brie had never been like this, even with Preston, but something about Alec made her want to let her guard down. Maybe it was because he'd seen her at her weakest and most vulnerable because of the plane crash, but he still wanted her.

"I would love that." Alec flicked his tongue along the shell of her ear and a zing of pleasure went straight to her womb.

"Tell me how it starts," he said in that deep voice with that accent which made her instantly wet.

"I was facing away from you." She turned in his arms to face the bed. "And I put my hands on the counter when you put your finger inside me."

Alec moved behind her with his hand between her legs to thrust a finger into her waiting wetness. She gasped, clenching tight as sensations exploded through her.

His other hand gripped her hip possessively. "Then what?"

"You pulled my jeans down and took me from behind."

He groaned again, the sound half pleasure, half tortured. "Yes. I would definitely do that." He put his hand on her back, pushing her down over the edge of the bed. Then he tugged her bottoms and panties down to her knees. Brie's breasts rubbed against the bed comforter with delicious friction as she wiggled her bottom in invitation. He unzipped his jeans and she closed her eyes as his cock nudged at her entrance. This was the most exciting thing she'd done in years.

"You ready for me?" Alec asked.

"Uh huh."

He thrust hard, filling her so fast she cried out. It was like last night, only *better*. She rubbed her face against the comforter and fisted her hands into the soft fabric. Alec rode her slow and hard, each movement bringing them closer to that singular powerful connection. As they moved together, their panting breaths and the creaking of the bed were the only sounds in the room.

The climax came for her first, hitting her like an avalanche and softening into slow, echoing waves of pleasure. Alec came moments later, whispering her name in that husky voice of his. A flood of heat warmed her insides as he leaned over and kissed the back of her neck. He slowly pulled out of her and she immediately missed the feeling of him being connected to her.

"Stay," he said before he walked to the bathroom. He ran the water and returned with a warm washcloth to clean her. She blushed as she straightened and shimmied out of her panties and shorts and stood completely naked before him. His eyes gleamed with appreciation at her full nakedness.

"You're staying, right?" she asked hopefully, then regretted it because of the look on his face.

"Do you want me to?" The hesitation in his voice hurt her but she understood. He needed to keep his distance from her. It made sense. The longer he stayed here, the more of a chance they would be discovered together. Some part of her wanted to take that chance, as risky was it was.

"Please, it's just nicer to..." God, she realized she must sound needy and pathetic right now. But it had been years since she'd really been with a man and after last night, she'd gotten addicted to the feeling of being safe in someone's arms.

He removed his sweater and then his pants. "I'll stay." He wore only a pair of boxers underneath. "This okay?" he asked.

Brie nodded. She turned to her suitcase at the foot of the bed and hastily retrieved a fresh pair of panties and a T-shirt, then climbed in bed with him.

"It's strange to be sleeping in a different bedroom," he chuckled.

"I thought you didn't come here often." Brie said curiously. "You still have an assigned room?"

"Assigned? No, I've had the same bedroom since childhood. It just happens to have eighteenth century bedroom furniture and tapestries."

"No racecar sheets for you, huh?" She snuggled up against him, unable to deny the urge to cuddle against him.

"Racecar sheets? I wish I'd been born in America if that's what boys got to have growing up." Alec slid a hand under the sheets to stroke her thigh. It wasn't meant to be sexual, but rather a comforting stroke that felt intimate in a different way. It was like he'd done it to her thousand times before.

"I'm glad you were born here. I like you just the way you are. British and all."

"British and all?" His voice warmed her inside as she heard the laughter in his tone.

"Trust me. American girls fantasize about men like you."

He watched her curiously, a faint smile on his lips. "And why is that?"

"Partially the accent, of course. You can read a grocery list and it would make us swoon."

"Groceries eh? Let's see, bananas, eggs, butter, fish and chips, biscuits, marmalade⎯"

"Stop!" Brie giggled, pretending to be aroused.

"Pears, apples, bread, milk…" Alec murmured as he lowered his head to hers to steal a soft kiss. It burned with a sweetness that made her heart ache. Could a kiss unlock one's heart and soul? Right now, it felt like it.

She curled an arm around his neck, holding him to her as she kissed him back. It was so easy to get lost in him, yet she didn't feel lost. She felt as if she was running toward something, something that would save her…or maybe break her.

"Hmm… You do indeed swoon. I shall have to remember that and recite groceries more often." Alec nuzzled her nose with his before pulling away. "Are you tired?"

"A little. I just want to drift off to sleep while you're here. You can still leave if you want, once I'm asleep." She snuggled deeper against him, clutching him the way a child might their favorite stuffed animal, but she was deliciously exhausted and couldn't find it in herself to care.

"It's alright, I don't mind staying. I grew up in this house and know how to get around with the least amount of chances of being seen.

"Do you mind if I keep the light on? I want to read for a bit." He reached for the leather journal on the bedside table.

"Only if you read to me."

"That I can do." He opened the journal. "This was my grandfather's. My father wanted me to read it."

"Are you okay with that? I know his death was hard for you."

Alec nodded. "It was, but the things in these pages... It's like he's here with me."

"Then introduce me. Let me hear his story." Brie wanted to listen to Alec. It was part of the magic of Merryvale, this hunger for knowledge, to hear the stories of those who lived within these walls. Alec cleared his throat and began to read.

"'My father told me that to be the Earl of Merryvale I need to understand people, to know their hearts. I feel this means I must leave behind the comforts of this world here in England and see the greater world for what it is, not simply what I read about.

"'Now I stand beneath the African sun, feeling its hot rays beat down upon me as I visit Nairobi. Many young men my age go on safaris. They tour these lands with Maasai guides, but their goal is to end the lives of the beautiful creatures here.

"'To hunt, to kill, it gives them a sense of power. But the thought of it turns my stomach. Killing can be a necessity, but for sport alone it is an abomination. A person's true power lies in what they can provide for other creatures. If one gives another creature's life the respect it deserves and leaves it in its place in the tapestry of life, they soon learn the truth of life, and their own place within it.

"'I have met the Massai chief, Mingati, which means the 'fast one.' I was told this was a Maasai lion name, given to him after he killed a lion hunting in their village at night. It was an honor bestowed upon him, yet he was quick to point out that he only killed the lion to save his village, not for some non-existent claim to glory.

"'I walked with Mingati, and lived in his village, and shared food with his family, as well as the elders of his tribe. We drank fresh milk in gourds that Mingati called *calabash*. Above us, the stars numbered in the millions and shone so bright that it dazzled me. The stars back home seem muted thanks to the glow of our cities, but not here... Everything here is pure. Africa is the cradle of life. The source.

"'The Maasai welcomed me and I in turn found a

kinship with them. Their warriors stand tall and proud in bright red clothing. Intelligence and ferocity fill their eyes as they gaze upon the vast and dangerous land they call home. They have a deep sense of honor and love to laugh even as they carry their spears at the ready. They hold fast to their language and culture, believe in respecting the past, and do not fear keeping traditions. They face death in much the same way, with calm respect and bravery. Mingati has told me that tomorrow we will hunt poachers. The elephants on their lands have been targeted and it is up to them to stop the men who would kill for ivory. I can think of no greater duty than to stand by Mingati's side and defend the wildlife that fill these African planes with splendor...'"

Alec paused in reading and Brie stirred against him, sleepy but still awake.

"He really hunted poachers?" she asked.

"He did," Alec confirmed. "When I was little, he used to show me a pair of spears in his office. I knew they were from Africa. I often wondered if they came from the tribe he stayed with."

"I bet they did." Brie put a hand on Alec's chest, feeling his slow, steady heartbeat beneath her fingers.

"He used to sing odd songs to Morgan and me as children. We always thought they sounded like nonsense, but he told me they were songs he learned in Africa. I wish I'd listened to him. I wish I could remember the words more clearly. It's a faded memory now."

"Do you remember anything about it?"

"Only that he said the song was called *The Rainmaker*."

"*The Rainmaker...*" Brie echoed. She would do some research tomorrow. A lot of tribal music was being recorded online now in an attempt to preserve local cultures around the world. There was a small chance she might be able to find it.

"He loved Africa so much. He only ever stayed there the one time all those years ago, but it was in his blood." Alec brushed his fingertips over the page. "He often quoted H. Rider Haggard's Allan Quartermain novels to me. It looks like he has written some inside his journal here."

"What does it say?"

"'*Truth I shall be dead. So it is with us all. How many millions have lain as I lie, and thought these thoughts and been forgotten! — Thousands upon thousands of years ago they thought them, those dying men of the dim past, and thousands on thousands of years hence will their descendants think them and be in their turn forgotten. As the breath of the oxen in winter, as the quick star that runs along the sky, as a little shadow that loses itself in sunset, as I once heard a Zulu called Ingrasi put it, such as the order of our life, the order that passeth away.'"*

"That's beautiful," Brie said. "How often do we neglect to make our lives have meaning beyond the here and now. Even if we go on to be forgotten, it doesn't mean we shouldn't live." She was silent a long moment. "I was married before…too young. I made mistakes and it was hard to move past them, to look to the future when there was still so much pain from the past."

"Would you tell me about him?" Alec asked. "Your ex-husband?"

"You want to hear about him?" She didn't think any man would ever want to hear about a woman's ex.

"Yes." Alec brushed his fingertips along her jaw line, sending goosebumps down her arms.

"His name was Preston." Brie drew in a deep breath as the memories came back to her. "We met freshman year in college. He was an arrogant frat guy; you know the kind. And I was a bookworm from the honors college. We only met because his fraternity was across the street from my dorm I lived in."

"How did you meet?" Alec watched her with open interest.

"He was throwing water balloons at us 'nerds'

when we left our dorm for classes. One hit my friend, so I…sort of ran at him and tackled him to the ground.”

“I bet he didn’t see that coming,” Alec chuckled.

“Oh, he definitely saw that coming. He just didn’t believe it.” Brie giggled, the memory was less painful now as she shared it.

“But once he saw you, he fell hard.” Alec could imagine how irresistible she was to any man.

“And so did I. I have a soft spot for hot arrogant guys, apparently.” She lightly patted his chest.

“Arrogant? I should be offended, but it’s true. I was a bit of an arse on the plane.”

Brie pinched her thumb and forefinger in the air. “Just a bit.”

“So, you and Preston met in college. When did you marry?”

“One year later.”

“So soon?”

“I know. I know.” Brie felt silly just even saying it out loud. Looking back now, she saw how foolish that early marriage had been. “I must sound like an idiot.”

“Not really. You’re hardly the first person I’ve met that married young. And some are still together. How long did you stay married?”

Brie placed her palm back on his chest. “Just four years.”

"What happened?" Alec caressed her thighs under her covers in a way that made her feel so safe. She stopped that dangerous thought before it could run away with her.

"Probably what you'd expect. We married for lust, not love, but we were too foolish to realize that. We just drifted apart and realized there was nothing to keep us tethered to one another." She remembered all too well that feeling, a vast invisible current pulling at them until it was too late.

"I can't imagine what that was like for you," Alec said. "I've never been in love, never let myself have a serious relationship. My job makes things complicated."

Brie sensed there was more he left unsaid, but she didn't push him. It was amazing they were even having this much of a conversation. She'd never talked to Preston about her feelings.

"Alec, we both know this isn't going to go anywhere real. You've got your work and I'll be going back to the States. But there's nothing wrong with us having an actual connection, right? Make this more than just casual sex?" She knew she was probably asking too much, but the need to pretend, to have just a taste again of being with someone like this mattered too much not to ask. "I mean, we're both adults, and I don't know about you, but I think I need this. I need to believe I can go back and start over, you know? I've been holding myself back too long."

Alec nodded. "I think I know what you mean. A relationship with a built-in expiry date."

"Well that sounds a bit morbid, but yeah, maybe." Alec was silent a long while but when he did respond it was unexpected. "I could see that. Neither of us needs the pressure to make it into something more, but I do enjoy your company. I'd like to get to know you better. Yes, I'd say it's possible."

"I'd like that."

He lifted her chin up so he could kiss her softly. "Very well. You're mine, for a few more days." His smile was playful and possessive in a way that stirred her heart

She kissed him back. "And you belong to me, too."

They kissed for a long while, until Alec put the journal away and turned off the light.

Morgan wandered down the hall of the family wing and groaned as he realized he'd gone too far a few seconds after he turned the knob on his brother's room instead of his own.

"Sorry Alec," he muttered. But no reply came from the bed. That was odd. Alec was a light sleeper and usually woke at even the slightest sounds.

"Alec?" He called his brother's name again and still was met with silence.

"Alec, this isn't funny." He reached for the light switch; Morgan shielded his eyes briefly as he adjusted to the light. Then he stared at Alec's bed. Empty. Still made.

Morgan glanced at the antique clock hanging on the wall. Merryvale had over one hundred and seventy clocks in the house, all of which were kept perfectly in time by their very dedicated butler.

It was midnight. Alec should be here.

Retracing his steps, Morgan visited the previous places he'd seen Alec tonight: the library, the salon, the drawing room, their grandfather's study. They were all empty. Morgan crossed the hall to the opposite wing where the guests were staying.

Outside Thad's room, he caught whispers of Thad and Veronica talking to one another. Then he padded down to Brie's room. He raised his hand to knock but he heard the murmurs of voices from within. And the list of possible suspects was pretty damn narrow.

A slow smile spread across Morgan's face. So, his older brother and the American...

"Good for you, Alec," Morgan said to himself. But he knew Alec well enough to know that this little romance was likely to be temporary. He was that kind of person.

Or was he? Morgan smirked. Maybe what Alec needed was a nudge in the right direction.

It's time you look to the future, Alec. Even if you hate me for helping you get there.

10

Alec woke long before Brie. The sounds of the house stirring to life around him always woke him. The creak of the pipes in the walls as the water moved through them, the bustle of the staff as they started their day, the calls outside of the groundskeeper from where he walked the hunting dogs as part of their morning ritual. The dogs barked and nipped in excitement, the sound echoing off the windows of the bedroom. Pale winter light trespassed through the half open curtains, giving the windows and the space around them a milky glow.

Brie lay beside him, her soft breathing a reassuring rhythm. Her body was flush against his. Her soft skin carried a hint of vanilla and sex which made his blood hum. How different it was to share her bed knowing they didn't have to part ways, not just yet anyway. Alec wanted to snuggle her closer and keep her in bed all day. In another life, it might have been possible...

His gaze drifted across the expansive bedroom, back to the forest tapestry. Gold threads glinted in the eyes of the wolf, the reddish hue having faded in the light of dawn. The frightening intensity of the beast he'd remembered from his youth had changed somehow. Now he saw a creature of shadow who braved the light in order to watch over and protect his world. A hunter who had chosen to protect rather than hunt the innocent deer that had been sewn so delicately into the exquisite patterns of greenery in the forest.

Alec shifted and adjusted the covers a little. He knew he ought to get up and return to his own bed. His brother had a habit, even as a grown man, of coming into his room and disturbing him at the most inconvenient hours. The last thing he needed was for Morgan to find his bed empty.

"Brie, I've got to go back to my room. Come find me when you're ready for breakfast. I'll be downstairs."

She murmured an unintelligible, yet adorable, reply. He caressed her cheek with his lips and left a ghost of a kiss on her before he slipped away. He tucked the covers over her since cold drafts could still seep through the older window casings. After quickly dressing, he exited Brie's room, only to collide with someone right outside the door. Thad.

"Aha!" Thad hissed in boyish glee. "I knew it. I *knew* it."

Alec steadied himself with a grunt. "It's not what you think."

"Oh? And how do you know what I'm thinking?" Thad crossed his arms, grinning. Friends or not, Alec was resisting the urge to sock his friend right in his smug jaw.

"I know you, Thad. You always assume the worst about me and women."

"Actually, I'm hoping for the best." His friend's smug smile wasn't reassuring, however.

Alec dragged his friend into an empty bedroom across the hall from Brie's. "Get in here." He shot Thad a death glare, but his friend only found it amusing.

"You had me convinced that you didn't like Brie. Even when Veronica told you about her plan to hook Brie up with Morgan, you played it cool. You had me fooled. You *like* her." Thad drawled out the word "like" as though he were in primary school teasing his fellow classmate.

"Thad, you can't tell anyone about this. *Anyone.*"

His brows furrowed. "Not even Veronica? We don't keep any secrets from each other."

"This isn't your secret to share. It's mine and Brie's. We've decided to keep this casual and at the end of the week we're ending it."

Thad was no longer teasing. "Why? If it's a good thing between you, you should want to continue it."

"Thad, can you honestly see me giving up my career? I'd have to in order to have any decent long-lasting relationship. Brie doesn't want to either. The woman has no desire to be in a relationship. And if you tell Veronica, it will get back to my mum and that's the last bloody thing we want. She could lose her job if her publisher found out."

Thad held up his hands in surrender. "Fine. Mum's the word, mate."

"Good." Alec relaxed slightly. He trusted Thad to keep his word once he gave it.

"Word of advice, Alec. Set an alarm and sneak out of her bedroom much earlier. Some of us wake early these days."

"Why are you awake? It's only six."

"Lyra and cartoons. It's our manly ritual to eat breakfast and watch them together."

"Ahh." Alec couldn't believe Thad had taken so well to being a dad to the girl but he had. If Alec hadn't known better, he would have assumed that Thad was the girl's biological father.

"You're welcome to join us," Thad offered.

"I might. I need to shower and change first though." He ran a hand over his slightly wrinkled sweater.

"Good idea. Best to get your walk of shame over with." Thad chuckled.

Alec flipped him off, though he smiled doing it.

They stepped back into the hallway and parted, Thad heading downstairs and Alec back to his room to shower. By the time he was ready for the day, he checked his phone and winced. Over seven missed calls from the office and thirty emails glared at him in bold font about the new transaction he was supposed to handle. Alec collected his iPad and headed down to the dining room.

Lyra, Thad and Morgan were all gathered around the tablet, which was propped up and streaming cartoons. The three of them laughed as they ate fresh blackberry scones and porridge.

"Morning." Morgan said, a hint of amusement in his voice that Alec chose to ignore. His little brother had a habit of finding even the most unamusing things funny, especially if they somehow irritated Alec.

Alec settled into a chair and one of the footmen brought him a bowl of porridge. "Morning."

"Thank you." He nodded at the young man who returned to the kitchens.

Alec spent his breakfast working and ignoring the trio at the other end of the table. He got the transaction started, gave his notes on the various elements that the lawyers would need to handle, and then pulled up the Wall Street Journal on his tablet and started scanning the articles. Even though he was a London investment banker, it was important to keep a global perspective in mind. Barclay's conducted business on multiple continents.

After that, he caught up on his emails, those about the current project and those from his clients about raising capital to help them grow their businesses. Emails completed, he now noticed the dining room was full. He checked his watch and realized he'd been working for almost two hours. It was just after nine.

"Alec, will you be joining us for sledding?" his mother asked hopefully.

Alec kept his focus on his mother, but casually managed to eye Brie as well. "Er... Yes. I suppose I can."

"Good." His mother stood. "Everyone be sure to dress warmly. We had fresh snow this morning and it's nippy outside."

The entire group gathered in the hall where coats, scarves, hats and mittens were distributed. Alec lingered close to Brie but kept the distance between as much as he could to avoid suspicion.

Once everyone was bundled up, they headed outside. Fresh snow almost a foot deep blanketed the landscape. Pepper led the way, the proud English lab perfectly able to high-step through the deep snow. Copper leapt in and out, creating little dents in the snow each time he landed. Yogi just simply plowed through the snow, forging his own path, which made Brie laugh. Alec found himself smiling along with her as the bulldog trudged ahead like a white and brown boulder rolling his way down a hill.

The groundskeeper, Mr. Grange, met them halfway to the nearest tall hill with a wood sled. He was a short, wiry fellow and Alec listened as he explained the history of Merryvale's lands to their guest. Brie held her small notebook and would pause to write notes every couple of steps. By the time the party reached the main sledding hill, Lyra was practically bouncing in excitement.

Thad lay down a large black toboggan and pulled Lyra onto it, having her sit in front of him. Veronica gave them a push and the sled shot down the hill to whoops and cheers until it slid to stop nearly two hundred yards away.

"That's a big hill," Brie said.

Julia grinned. "It is. It's been used for sledding for almost a hundred years."

Byron and Mr. Grange set two more toboggans down. "Who's next?"

"I will go." Morgan clasped Brie's hand and pulled her onto the front of the nearest toboggan. "And so will Brie!"

"Hold on, Morgan." Alec started toward them, but his brother laughed.

"Too late!" Morgan leapt up on the sled behind Brie who gasped and clutched the sides of the sled as it rocketed down the hillside. Alec glowered at his brother's quickly retreating form. The sled hit a patch of ice halfway down the hill and suddenly increased in speed. Alec was rooted in place as he watched the sled head straight for the trees.

"They're going too fast!" He shouted as he finally jerked his legs in the motion.

"Oh God!" His mother cried out, but Alec was sprinting down the hill, desperate to reach them but it was too late. The sled collided with a large cedar trunk and the distant figures hit the tree before collapsing into the snow.

Alec nearly fell down the hill trying to catch up. Lyra and Thad, who had only just started back up the hill, got there a moment before Alec did.

"Morgan?" Thad rolled Morgan onto his back. Morgan groaned and tried to sit up.

"Stay down." Thad pressed a hand to his shoulder keeping him flat on the snow.

Alec knelt beside Brie and mimicked Thad's motions to carefully roll her over. "Brie, darling, talk to me." Her eyes were closed, and there was a nasty gash over her forehead.

"Thad!" Alec gasped. "She's bleeding."

"Hang on." Thad asked Morgan a series of questions: the day, the year, his name, who the prime minister was, then checked Morgan's eyes using a pin flashlight from his coat pocket. Only when he seemed satisfied did he come to Alec and Brie.

"It looks bad," Alec whispered, looking at the blood.

"Head wounds bleed. It doesn't mean she's hurt badly." Thad checked her pulse against his wristwatch and lifted her eyelids and flashed the pin light. Brie groaned, her eyes blinking against the light.

"Brie, how many fingers do you see?" Thad held up his index finger.

"One?"

"And now?" He held up three fingers at a slight angle from her vision.

"Three." Brie's eyes drifted from Thad over to Alec. "Alec...I don't feel so good." Without warning, she rolled over and vomited on the snow. Alec held her shoulder, trying to do anything he could to comfort her.

"That's a sign of a concussion." Thad was frowning in deep worry now.

"Should she go to the hospital?" Alec asked.

"We can take her," Byron offered while Julia, Mr. Grange, and Veronica looked on with concern.

"Let me get a better look at her wound first, then we can take her." Thad gently touched the area around the cut.

"No signs of major trauma, but she should get an MRI just in case." Alec gently clasped Brie's hand in his while Thad completed his examination.

"Father, get the car ready. I'll carry Brie." Alec pulled her into the cradle of his arms and started the trek up the long, steep hill. Veronica and Thad helped Morgan to his feet and collected the sleds to return them to the house. Lyra followed beside Alec.

"Is she gonna be okay?" Lyra asked in a quiet voice.

"She'll be fine," Alec replied.

"I'll be fine," Brie echoed, trying to smile, but her lips seemed too weak to hold it for long.

"Hold on, darling," Alec murmured to her.

"Okay, I'm just going to close my eyes." Brie's eyes shut and Alec sped up his pace. By the time he reached the house, his father had the car on, the heater running, and the passenger doors wide open. Alec climbed inside, Brie on his lap and Thad took the front passenger seat.

The drive to the nearest ER seemed to take forever. The entire time he kept his gaze on Brie's face and the bloody handkerchief he held pressed to her forehead. A strange sense of panic threatened to choke him. She was going to be okay, he knew that logically, but it didn't stop him from inventing terrible scenarios in his head. His stomach clenched with a pulsing fear as they finally reached the hospital. Thad hurried into the ER and returned with a gurney just as Alec got out. The nurses rolled her into the ER, with Thad and Alec following right behind. Alec felt helpless as she was taken into a room for tests.

"May I go with her?" he asked the attending doctor.

"You need to stay outside." The woman pointed toward an observation window. "But you can watch her through there."

"Thank you." Alec pressed his palm to the glass and watched as nurses moved Brie onto the MRI machine's bed and helped her dress into a hospital gown.

"She'll be fine, Alec." Thad joined Alec at the window.

"You sure?" he asked.

"I've seen plenty of concussions. This is just a precaution."

Still, he couldn't tear his eyes away from her.

Thad leaned against the window. "Alec, I've never seen you like this with a woman before."

Alec said nothing.

"Alec, how did this thing between you two start?"

Alec tried to brush it off. "Doesn't matter."

"Was it because of the crash? The plane crash, I mean."

That caught Alec's attention. "If it was, does that matter? We had to share a bed. We were both stressed out. Things just happened."

Thad's usually teasing expression was serious. "Alec, you need to be careful. Take it from someone who knows all about Florence Nightingale Syndrome. People bond in situations like that, attachments are made, but the relationships born don't usually last. Not romantically, anyway. You get together for all the wrong reasons."

"We aren't *together*. It's just a tryst." The word tasted like a lie, but it was the truth. They'd promised this week together had a built in expiry date. No expectations. No regrets.

"If you say so…" Thad sighed. "Because right now you're acting like a man whose heart is breaking as he watches a woman he's fallen in love with be in pain. I know what you're going through. You feel helpless. You can't do anything but wait."

Alec leaned until his forehead rested against the glass of the observation window. "I know."

Thad put a hand on his shoulder and didn't say anything else.

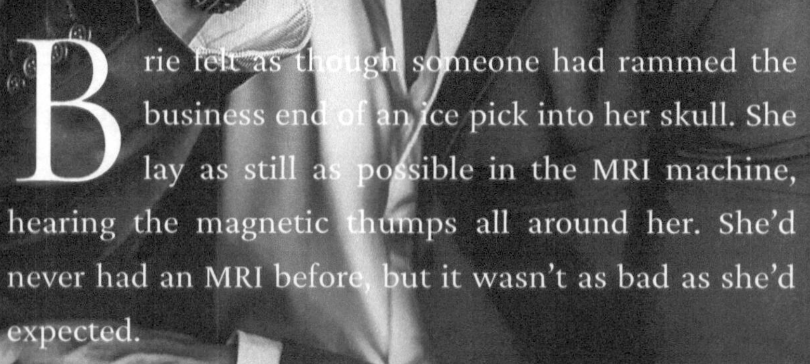

11

Brie felt as though someone had rammed the business end of an ice pick into her skull. She lay as still as possible in the MRI machine, hearing the magnetic thumps all around her. She'd never had an MRI before, but it wasn't as bad as she'd expected.

"You're all done." The nurse rolled her out of the sanitized white tunnel. "Can you sit up? I'll help you into a wheelchair."

Wheelchair? This was a sledding accident, not a car crash. Brie's humiliation was rising, especially when she saw Alec and Thad watching her through an observation window a dozen feet away. She climbed off the table and saw Alec give a halfhearted wave as she was eased into the wheelchair. Her neatly folded clothes were placed in her lap and the nurse wheeled her into the hallway where Alec and Thad joined them.

"You okay, Brie?" Thad asked.

She nodded. "I just have a killer headache."

Alec said nothing but he kept pace with the wheelchair as they headed to an exam room. The nurse left the three of them alone and Thad pulled out his cell.

"I'll be right back. I'm going to give Veronica an update and see if your dad parked the car."

"Thanks." Alec turned to Brie once they were alone. He knelt in front of her, bracing his hands on either side of her arms. "I'm glad you're okay."

"I guess I wrecked sledding, huh?" Her voice held regret and Alec's intense hazel eyes softened.

"No, that was Morgan's fault. He shouldn't have put two adults on that hill in one sled. Your combined weight on the ice only increased your speed."

"Is Morgan okay? I was pretty out of it after the crash." Bits and pieces flashed across her mind. The excitement of flying down the hill, the hard ice beneath the sled, rushing into the forest, the crack of plastic, her muffled scream and blinding pain, then nothing.

"He's fine. He's worried about you, but fine." Alec held her chin, examining her.

"Alec..." She opened her mouth to say more but the doctor entered with Thad right behind her. The doctor, a dark-haired woman in her forties, performed several tests on her, then cleaned and examined her cut.

"A minor concussion. I recommend rest and relaxation. Don't do any hard work, physical or mental for a week. Enjoy the holidays. If your headache worsens, please come back straightaway." She bandaged up the cut. "Treat the wound once a day with fresh antibiotic cream and bandages. It should heal in no time."

"Thanks." Brie exhaled in relief. She wanted to go home and rest.

She glanced toward Alec, and tried to smile, but it came out weary and half-hearted. Alec put an arm around her shoulder, not caring if anyone saw, and for some reason that simple gesture made her want to cry. He'd carried her all the way up the hill, like a hero from her romance novels and he'd stayed with her. His presence offered a comfort that she hadn't felt in years. It had been so long since she'd had anyone looking after her, that Brie had forgotten what it felt like to be cared about. She covered one of Alec's hands with hers and closed her eyes as he squeezed her hand back.

Thad returned a minute later. "I found your dad, Alec. He's in the lobby. We'll go pull the car up and you can bring Brie outside."

Brie was glad to leave the wheelchair and exam table behind. Byron had the car pulled up right outside the entrance. Alec escorted her to the back seat so she could sit beside him.

Byron smiled at her from the rearview mirror. "You look much better, Ms. Honeyweather."

"I'm feeling better."

"Good. I'm glad to hear it."

By the time they reached the house it was late afternoon and the great hall had dozens of new guests, including five children around Lyra's age. Julia spotted them as they entered the hall and rushed over.

"Brie, dear, how do you feel?"

"I'm fine. Really."

"She needs to rest and have a bit of quiet," Alec interjected, hovering close to her.

"Then someone should stay with her," Julia said. "Everyone else go on, Brie and I will have some downtime here. We can discuss our book."

"But you'll miss the village fair," Byron reminded her. "The patrons for the fundraiser are expecting you."

"Oh yes, you're right..."

"I would really like to go," Brie insisted.

"Heavens, no, dear. You must rest and you shouldn't be alone. Even with the staff here, I wouldn't allow it. Alec, be a dear and keep her company, would you? The rest of us need to go down to the village this afternoon. We'll be back after dinner."

Alec agreed without hesitation. Brie shot him a warning look, but he ignored it. He escorted her to her room, where she changed out of her heavy clothes and into a comfortable pair of jeans and a navy-blue crewneck sweater.

"So, what are we going to do while everyone's gone to the fair?" she asked Alec. He leaned back against her bed with his arms folded as he studied her intently. His hazel eyes seemed to hold a thousand secrets.

"I thought we could read by the fire, perhaps roast chestnuts. Nothing too taxing."

Even though Brie didn't feel up to it, she was disappointed he hadn't mentioned sex. Alec's lips twitched in a hint of a smile. "I saw that." Sensual delight lingered in his words.

"What?"

"You want me to say it?"

She didn't respond with an answer.

"Brie, I would love nothing more than to strip you bare and take you right now, but that doesn't qualify as rest. The sooner you heal, the sooner we can break the headboard of this lovely Jacobean bed." He knocked his knuckles lightly against a bedpost.

Brie walked over to him, standing close enough that she could feel the energy simmering between them. "Promise?"

It had been easy to become addicted to Alec's rich voice, the warm ochre color of his eyes, and the way he touched her. But the best, and the most dangerous part, was how he made her feel. Like she mattered, like she was desired, like he wanted her to be a part of his life. It made no sense; they were barely friends, yet there was such a strong connection between them that was irresistible.

But lust and desire could mimic a lot of other emotions. She made that mistake before.

"I promise." Alec gripped her hips. His gaze held a mixture of tenderness and desire that made her heart flutter. He flashed a devastating grin as he lowered his head and kissed her. Blood surged from her fingertips to her toes and a hot ache grew in her throat as she longed for more.

He gently clasped her to him, her softer curves molded to the firm contours of his body. His palm slid from her hips to explore the hollow of her back. She'd never felt like this before. Even the act of being held in his arms and kissing him was all she would ever need in life.

When their lips finally parted, she felt the burning sweetness it left behind and shyly touched her lips with her fingertips. Alec's mouth relaxed in a lazy smile. This was the Alec she liked, the man who, in that moment, was not a workaholic investment banker. He was simply a man, a gorgeous one at that, and he was all *hers*. Merryvale was their private refuge, a place where she could forget her past and he forget his bleak future, at least for a brief span of time.

She didn't want to think about how soon it would all end, like the snow melting away in the early spring.

"Why don't you grab a notebook and pen? I'll show you some of my favorite things about Christmas before you rest for a bit."

"Okay." As she followed him into the hall, she became lost in the magic of his words and the way his face lit up when he talked about his home.

"In late September, the light starts to change. Autumn slowly turns the landscape gold. The farmers harvest their crops and Merryvale begins to stock its larder with all that we'll need for the long cold winter. We tour the village during its annual Christmas fair on Christmas Eve. The money raised at the fair is donated to a charity of my mother's choice every year."

"What's the charity this year?" Brie asked. The excited crowd of new guests for the holidays had departed the great entryway, leaving it quiet once more. The marble busts tucked in alcoves wearing their holly crowns watched in silence as Alec and Brie descended the stairs.

"I believe this year the donations go toward our troops. Mom will arrange for care packages." Alec paused at the bottom of the stairs. "Smell that?" He grinned and held out a hand. Brie hesitated, until she remembered no one was here to see. Following the maze of rooms and hallways, Alec led her back to the kitchens, where they'd baked cookies the day before. The cooks were now preparing mince pies, soups, Christmas quiches and various beautifully iced cakes.

"Christmas at Merryvale is a blend of ancient rituals and modern customs. We strive to show the beauty of the land around us, so we don't lose the heritage that makes this place unique. The cooks base our menus around what is grown and harvested in the fall, typically winter fruits and special cuts of meat." Alec grinned as he stole a blackberry tart and handed it to Brie. Then he stole one for himself before they exited the kitchens.

"On Christmas morning, a host of local bagpipe players will stand outside and play Highland Christmas songs."

"Bagpipes?" Brie bit into the blackberry tart, the slick sugar coating was like liquid honey upon her tongue.

"Oh, yes. You'll like it, I think." Alec finished his tart before taking her hand again. He guided her through a series of rooms and Brie marveled at all the books she saw. Piles by beds, by desks, and baskets near couches, and the library itself glowed with gilded spines. Merryvale was a wealth of stories about people and places.

"My grandfather was as great believer in the power of books," Alec said.

Brie laced her fingers through his as they gazed up at the vast expanse of titles. "So am I."

"Books always seemed to glow, don't they?" Alec mused. "The way the light catches on the spines. You can almost see the stories within them like a halo.

"They do," Brie agreed. She'd marveled at that same thing before while in the middle of some old bookshop where she'd passed by a shelf near a window and the light illuminated a specific spine. It was like the book was calling to her in an almost magical way.

"If you feel up to it, we can take a walk in the snow," Alec offered.

"I'd like that. I'm not feeling too bad."

Once dressed for the weather, they left the house. Brie looked back at the front door. The tall walnut wood was heavily oiled, weathered, and studded with iron-mongered bits; it was also festively decorated with two matching Christmas wreaths. She knew from her research that the shape was no accident. The circular shape represented eternity, with no beginning or end, and the evergreen making up the wreaths symbolized eternal life. It brought a symbolic beauty to the sight.

Alec led her down a path of trees. The slender gray trunks of the birch bent slightly in the wintry breeze and felt like ghostly guardians.

"My grandfather called these ghost chasers. He said that birch trees would ward off evil." Alec placed a gloved hand on the smooth, white bark that was knotted with black spots like a thousand eyes. Beyond the forest, a field of pure white snow covered the earth.

"I used to love it here," Alec said. "I loved everything about this place." He squeezed her hand slightly as he met her worried gaze. "But it's hard to look upon now. It only reminds me of what I've lost."

"The more you look at it, the more you should remember the good, not the bad." Brie moved closer to him. "After my parents died, I hid the pictures, tucked them into drawers or cabinets. But the pain stayed anyway. Later on, I took the pictures back out and the good memories began to outweigh the pain of what was gone."

Alec leaned his head down to hers, their foreheads touching. "How is it that you always know the right thing to say? How are you so wise?" He closed his eyes, holding onto her mitten-covered hands as their breath mingled in the air around them.

"I guess I'm just amazing." She deadpanned the reply, winning a smile from him.

"You are such an American," he chuckled and kissed her. "Come on, just a bit farther."

They walked through the fresh snow down the tunnel of birch trees until they reached a small clearing. An angel carved of stone wept above a tombstone.

Snow-capped, her head and her wings draped over the headstone, protecting it. The name *Walter Halston* was carved into the stone along with the words, *"I desire to live worthily as long as I have lived, and to leave after my life, to the great men who should come after me, the memory of me in good works."* — *Alfred the Great.*

Ivy climbed around the statue, but its leaves had fallen away, leaving a gnarled patchwork of roots and vines gripping the stone. Bursts of color stood out among the dead ivy. Winter berries, spindle plants, and red-berried holly thrived in the absence of the over-powering ivy leaves.

"He wanted to be buried here on the land, rather than in the churchyard." Alec's voice grew rough. "I haven't been back here since the funeral."

"It's peaceful," she said, reassuring him. It hurt her to know that he was reliving something that had wounded him so deeply.

"My grandfather was the only one who seemed to

understand me. He was different than the rest of my family. He understood me in ways I can't really explain. Don't misunderstand me, I love my family. But my grandfather and I...we had a special bond. I don't know if that even makes sense."

It did. Brie bit her lip. She felt at home with Alec in a way she'd only ever felt around her parents. But even with them, she'd felt isolated. Even when she'd only known the rude and arrogant Alec on the plane, she'd still felt engaged, alive, and focused when she was near him. It hadn't been like that with Preston, not really. She knew she would never would have had a conversation like this with her ex-husband.

ALEC LOOKED AROUND THE CLEARING AT HIS GRANDFATHER'S grave as he squeezed Brie's hand. "I'm glad you came."

"Here? Or Merryvale?"

"Both."

"Me too." She leaned into his touch. "I'm glad you came home for Christmas."

Alec looked once more upon his grandfather's tombstone and blinked in surprise. The brown vines blanketing the base of the monument looked greener now, didn't they? He had to be imagining it. He grew up hearing about the magic of Merryvale, but he never believed in it, at least not fully.

But maybe...maybe he should believe in it. Magic didn't have to be about wizards and spells. Sometimes it was a quiet snowy afternoon with a person who made you feel whole again.

He gently touched the skin above the cut on her forehead. "Let's get you back inside. You should rest."

"Maybe you could teach me to roast chestnuts? I've always wanted to learn."

"Absolutely."

They returned to the house, holding hands. It would be hours before the others returned and they would have to go back to hiding their relationship. They removed their coats and returned to the kitchens, sitting at a small table in the corner. The cooks had prepared a quick meal of turkey, brie, and cranberry sandwiches on rye bread.

"I'm finally getting to eat you after all," Alec whispered in her ear. She kicked him in the shin but also laughed.

"Why is my name so funny to you?" she demanded but she couldn't stop giggling.

"It's a *cheese*. It's hilarious."

She rolled her eyes and licked cranberry sauce off her fingers. "Okay, show me your nuts then."

Alec choked on his sandwich. "My *nuts*?"

She leaned into him and caressed his thigh. "Your *chestnuts*."

He laughed so hard that it actually hurt his ribs. He hadn't laughed like that since... He honestly couldn't remember.

"Seriously, show me how to roast chestnuts."

Still chuckling, he collected their plates and put them in the sink before he retrieved a bag of large shiny chestnuts from the pantry and set it on one of the counters.

"Lesson one. You don't use horse chestnuts; those are for decoration. You want to get the nuts from an 'eating tree.' Chestnuts were a great source of carbohydrates in the winter during the middle ages, hence the tradition of roasting them on an open fire."

"Like the Nat King Cole song."

"Exactly." Alec turned the oven on. "You want the oven to be 200°C or 400°F for the Americans in the room." He set out a roasting tray and started cutting a slit into each chestnut. He placed the nuts flat side down on the tray, then slid the tray into the oven.

"You should cook them for approximately thirty minutes, or until you see the skin crack farther apart. Once it's done you allow them to cool, then peel away the shell to reveal the brown membrane. Then you can eat them."

He closed the oven door and set the timer.

"So, we have thirty minutes. Whatever shall we do?" Brie asked, letting her gaze wander along his body. It made him hard all over, but he had to resist. With a concussion, rest was crucial, and he wasn't about to be selfish. But he knew she was hoping for a distraction, so he came up with a way to do just that.

"I could show you my non-racecar sheets," Alec offered a low seductive tone. Her eyes sparkled with excitement.

"That sounds like a great idea," Brie replied, her voice slightly breathless.

Alec told the cooks to watch the oven time for them and held out his hand. Brie placed her palm in his. He felt like a boy with his first crush.

They stopped in front of his room a minute later and a flutter of nerves filled his chest. He opened the door and glanced around, wondering what she would think of it. She walked in ahead of him and paused by the large windows overlooking the forest beyond. Alec joined her, curling an arm around her waist.

"In the spring I see the fallow deer in the clearing below. The little fawns stumble about all knock-kneed. It's so bloody cute."

Brie's lips curved in a dreamy smile. "The life you have here is special. I hope you realize that, Alec. All of this is a gift."

He knew she was right, but right now *she* felt like the real gift.

She turned back to his bed and ran exploring finger-tips over the medieval style headboard of his four poster. Lions, unicorns, and heraldry shields were intricately embedded and painted with a master's touch. The dark crimson coverlet glowed with hints of gold from the light of the early evening sun.

"So, show me those non-racecar sheets," Brie teased.

Alec pulled back the covers to expose pale gold sheets instead. He sensed weariness in her eyes. His real goal in getting her here had been to get her to rest. He had no plans for anything more until she was better, but she didn't have to know that.

"Lie down on your stomach. I'll give you a massage," he offered.

"Okay." She blushed before she removed her brown ankle boots and climbed into the bed. Something inside him puffed with pride at seeing her in his bed.

He knelt beside her and began to massage her neck and shoulders. The soft sounds of pleasure that came from her made him grin, but within minutes she was asleep, just as he'd planned. He settled next to her and pulled her into the curve of his body as he let himself relax. Soon, he, too, started to drift off.

Movement caught his attention as a falcon landed on the balcony outside his window. It's brown and cream-colored feathers ruffled as the bird of prey relaxed for a brief moment.

That was how Alec felt. This slice of holiday paradise was but a brief moment to catch his breath before he had to face the challenges of the world again.

If only I could stay here with her forever. It would be a much simpler life...

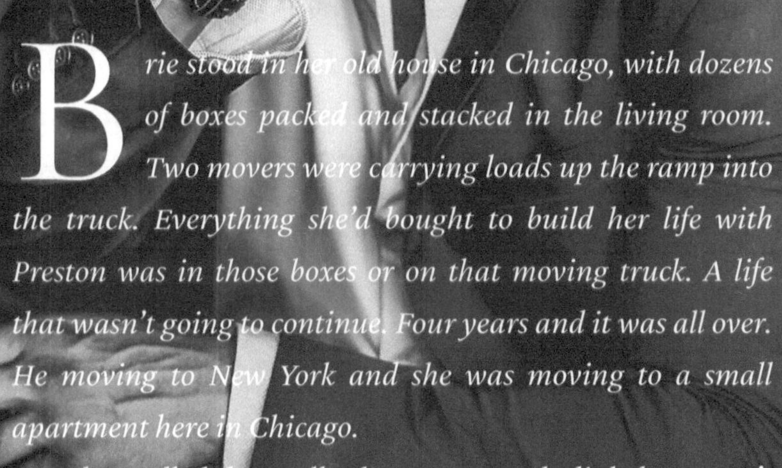

12

Brie stood in her old house in Chicago, with dozens of boxes packed and stacked in the living room. Two movers were carrying loads up the ramp into the truck. Everything she'd bought to build her life with Preston was in those boxes or on that moving truck. A life that wasn't going to continue. Four years and it was all over. He moving to New York and she was moving to a small apartment here in Chicago.

She pulled her cell phone out and dialed Preston's number. He answered after four rings.

"Hey."

"Hey," she echoed softly. Somehow in the last four years they'd become strangers again.

"The stuff should be all packed in a few hours. You sure you don't want anything?" she asked.

"No, it's all right. My assistant can furnish my new apartment. It's cheaper than trying to get the stuff from Chicago to Manhattan."

"Oh right, that makes sense." Brie's throat felt like she'd swallowed glass. There was something painful about knowing that Preston didn't want anything from their once shared life.

"You want any photos?" she asked after a minute.

"I don't think that's a good idea. We both agreed we needed a fresh start."

Brie had always hated that phrase, "a fresh start." It made her feel like what they'd before had turned rotten. It hadn't. It had simply fizzled out like a flame fluttering in the darkness until a final gust of wind snuffed it out.

"So..." She didn't want to hang up. To end the call meant it was well and truly over.

"So...my assistant mailed you the divorce papers. Sign them when you get the chance, okay?" Preston's tone was gentle, almost hesitant, as if he sensed what she did.

"Preston, we're doing the right thing, aren't we?" She didn't want to be the one who gave up on their marriage, but she couldn't see any other way forward for either of them.

"I think so." Preston sighed in the phone and the sound cut her heart with fresh pain. "We weren't really happy. We were just...coasting, you know?" She could hear him tap on *his desk and pictured the way he leaned back in his chair, drumming his fingers as he talked. She knew so much about him, but that hadn't been enough. Knowing someone wasn't the same as loving them.*

Brie closed her eyes and leaned against the living room wall. "I guess we were."

"I wish..." Preston began.

"What?" She opened her eyes and held her breath.

"I wish we had known then what we know now. We were just kids." Preston's rueful tone made tears well up in her eyes.

"We were. Kids who thought we knew what love was."

Love wasn't flowers and roses. Love was fights late into the night. It was holding one another as you faced a devastating loss. It was a stone wall against a raging sea. It wasn't easy and it wasn't always full of sunshine and sweet but empty promises. Love was knowing that no matter what, the other person had your back and you had theirs, even through pain and heartache.

"Take care of yourself, Brie."

"You too."

Preston hung up. Brie dropped her phone and broke down in silent, body wracking sobs.

The dream, or rather the memory, slowly faded at the edges like an old photograph left too long in the sun. When she was finally free of it, she blinked. Her eyes were thick with tears and her head throbbed. She'd been crying in her sleep.

Then she remembered where she was and who she was with. Alec's warm breath teased her neck as she lay beside him. At least she hadn't woken him up. She could only imagine what he'd make of her current state. She carefully slid his arm off her waist and slipped out of the bed. She bent, retrieved her boots, and left the room. She needed some Tylenol and some time to think.

God, had she really been dreaming about Preston? She hadn't done since they year they separated. Alec was bringing back too many painful memories. Maybe she wasn't ready for this. She didn't trust herself to know when what she was feeling was more than just simple attraction. Brie found two Tylenol in her room and ran a glass of water in the bathroom to swallow them before she exited her bedroom.

"Brie?" Veronica called her name from near the stairs.

"Hey." She smiled at her friend. "You guys back from the fair already?"

"Yep," Veronica pulled Brie into the light a little more. "How's your head?"

"You are such a mom sometimes." Brie laughed. "It hurts a little. I took some Tylenol."

"Good, that should help, but if the headache doesn't go away by tomorrow, you need to let Thad know, okay?"

"Okay." Brie sighed. "Did you get any pictures from the fair for me? I'm so upset I missed it." Julia had described the local fair as the highlight of the Christmas season in the Merryvale area.

"We did. I've got tons of pictures. I even took some notes for you." Veronica handed her a small notebook. It bore the Halston family crest with the gold embossed logo of Merryvale Court. "I bought this at the little gift shop here."

Brie glanced at the diligent notes. "This is so great. Seriously, thank you, Veronica."

"You're welcome. Why don't you come down and eat some roasted chestnuts with me?"

Brie glanced over her shoulder toward Alec's room and did her best to bury the dream she'd had of Preston. It was Christmas Eve and she had work to do. She couldn't think about the past...or about a future with Alec.

Alec woke to a cold, empty bed. He raked a hand through his hair, confused, and stared about his bedroom.

"Brie?" he looked toward the bathroom, but the door was open. She wasn't in there.

Was she okay? He sat up and threw his covers back hastily before he put his boots on and started toward the door. He reached it just as it swung open and almost hit him in the face.

"There you are," Morgan said. He was still wearing his coat and seemed to be shifting restlessly.

"What's the matter with you?" Alec asked his brother. He wasn't just squirming, something seemed to be moving inside his chest. If it wasn't for the fact Morgan was laughing, he'd have thought an alien might burst out any moment.

"Alec you owe me big...*so* big." Morgan unzipped his heavy coat and pulled a small chocolate colored cocker spaniel pup from his coat. It wriggled and whimpered, its large silky ears as big as it's adorable little head.

"I can't bring that back to my London flat," Alec said flatly. This was another one of Morgan's bizarre schemes, he just didn't understand why his little brother was giving him a dog.

"She's not for you. She's for Brie."

"What? Why?" Alec demanded. "Do you have any

idea the trouble you've caused already with the sled? She has a concussion, Morgan."

Morgan's devious expression faded. "I'm sorry about that, Alec. But here's the thing. I'm not giving her the dog. *You* are." He pushed the puppy into Alec's chest. Alec grabbed the puppy on reflex. It snuggled into his hands and yawned widely. Alec groaned in frustration.

"Morgan...what the bloody hell are you—?"

"Listen. When she first got here, she said she'd never had a dog because her first husband was allergic. It's clear she adores our dogs."

"Course she does. Our dogs are wonderful."

Morgan shook his head. "Only to dog lovers. I've brought several girls here over the years. Women who aren't dog lovers don't let Yogi climb on their laps. Trust me, that doesn't go over well with the others."

"That doesn't mean Brie wants a dog. She may simply *like* dogs. And why should I be the one to give it to her?"

Morgan stared at him, unimpressed. "Because you're shagging her, of course."

Alec said nothing. He wasn't sure what to say. Had Thad broken his word? Was Morgan just guessing?

"And you *like* her."

"I'm not shagging her," Alec said flatly.

"Oh? Then where were you last night? I walked into your bedroom this morning and it was empty."

"I stayed up late reading in the library."

Morgan expression was nonplussed. "Try again. I checked there next. Not a sight or sound of you to be found anywhere, except for one room…"

"Morgan, whatever game you think you're playing, stop now. Brie will be in a lot of trouble with her publisher if they find out she's in a relationship with her client's son," Alec warned.

"Ah, so you admit it's a relationship?" Morgan grinned, as if that was what the proof he'd been waiting for.

"Christ, it's like talking to a brick wall." Alec walked around his brother and stepped into the hall. "Where did you even get this thing?" He nodded down at the spaniel as Morgan caught up with him.

"One of the farmers at the fair had a litter. She has papers and everything. She's a fine dog."

"She's cute," Alec grudgingly admitted. "She's what, barely eight weeks old?" He stroked a finger down the puppy's nose and a little pink tongue slipped out to lick his finger.

"Nine, actually. Runt of the litter, but I figured that just adds to the charm. Now, you need to get a big bow, a good red or green one, and then give the puppy to Brie for Christmas tonight. Maybe tuck it in a hatbox or something."

"Like *Lady and the Tramp*? Morgan, my life is not a Disney movie."

"It could be if you wanted it to," Morgan muttered. "Just do it and you'll be a lucky man."

"It wouldn't be appropriate, Morgan."

"Oh, for God's sake. It's a puppy, not an engagement ring."

Alec paused at the top of the stairs and lifted the puppy up to look at it. The puppy tried to lick his nose. Alec sighed.

"You'd better go raid the extra pet supplies in the stables. You'll need a fresh bed, and a carrier."

"I've already seen to all of that," Morgan said. "And puppy food as well. It's all in the downstairs closet for when you're ready to give her to Brie."

Alec stopped one of their footmen, a man named Murphy, and entrusted him to care for the pup until later that night. The brothers then joined everyone in the main salon to enjoy some roasted chestnuts.

He saw Brie across the room with Veronica and his mother, but something felt wrong. Brie didn't look his way once. He moved through the crowd, dodging Lyra and the group of children she was playing with. He didn't wish to interrupt the conversation of the fair Brie was so fully engrossed in, so he waited instead for them to finish.

"Oh Alec! Did you let Brie sleep this afternoon?" His mother said when she noticed him hovering nearby. "She looks exhausted." Julia frowned at him then turned to Brie. "Tonight, we'll turn in early. Let the children finish the chestnuts and then Byron will perform his reading of *T'was the Night Before Christmas*."

Alec studied Brie's face and noted the wariness in her expression. When his mother and Veronica moved away, he sidled closer.

"Are you all right? You were gone when I woke."

"Yes, I'm fine." Brie focused on her notebook as she jotted down some things.

"What's the matter? I get the sense you're avoiding me," he said so as not to be overheard.

"Alec, we've been kidding ourselves. I know we're both adults and we're just having fun, but we need to stop before..." She trailed off.

"Before what?"

"Before one of us makes a mistake. I can't afford to do that, okay? Let's just call it quits now."

Logically her words make perfect sense, but for some reason it filled him with a deep pain, one that made it harder to breathe, like he'd run too fast outside in the cold, and his lungs were almost frozen. Brie started to walk away, but he caught her wrist, tugging her back toward him.

"Brie, please, I'm sorry if I said anything that made you uncomfortable. Please don't take this from me, give me a few more days with you."

Alec hadn't begged for anything in a long time. The last time he could remember doing it was when his grandfather had been rushed away in an ambulance. He'd prayed and *begged* for Walter not to die, that the paramedics had been wrong when they told his family to prepare for the worst. Prayers and begging the universe hadn't done anything back then.

"Alec...we both knew this was risky. I don't think I can do this for another few days."

"What changed? What happened between the moment you fell asleep in my arms and now?"

She was quiet a long moment before replying. "The truth? I had a bad dream. One that reminded me that my life isn't a fairytale. That life? The life I have hoped for ever since I was a girl? It doesn't exist." Her eyes were tense with pain.

"What doesn't exist?" Alec asked.

"Love." Her simple answer stunned him so greatly that when she pulled at her arm, he let her go. Her wrist slid out from his fingertips.

"Brie..." he whispered, but Brie was already crossing

the room, though she might as well have been at the opposite end of the universe.

EVERYONE SETTLED INTO THE COZY DRAWING ROOM. A roaring fire was lit, the flames crackling and popping on the logs. The children had all clustered near a large armchair where Byron wore a night robe and a floppy night cap and sat with an old leatherback book resting in his lap. Between his teeth was an old pipe which he puffed on dramatically even though no smoke came out. Brie watched the children giggle at his antics.

"He doesn't actually smoke it," Morgan murmured from beside her. "Too health-conscious, but the children love it all the same."

"Let me guess, you suggested using a bubble pipe, instead," said Brie as she noticed that bubbles were starting to come up out of the pipe's mouth.

"How did you know?"

"Call it a hunch." Brie found herself smiling, despite her heart aching after her talk with Alec.

Byron made a show of settling into his chair, then cleared his throat and opened the book.

'Twas the night before Christmas, when all through the house

Not a creature was stirring, not even a mouse;

The stockings were hung by the chimney with care,

In hopes that St. Nicholas soon would be there;

The children were nestled all snug in their beds;

While visions of sugar-plums danced in their heads;

And mamma in her 'kerchief, and I in my cap,

Had just settled our brains for a long winter's nap,

When out on the lawn there arose such a clatter,

I sprang from my bed to see what was the matter.

Away to the window I flew like a flash,

Tore open the shutters and threw up the sash.

The moon on the breast of the new-fallen snow,

Gave a lustre of midday to objects below,

When what to my wondering eyes did appear,

But a miniature sleigh and eight tiny rein-deer,"

Byron paused, letting the children gasp in suspense and the adults all chuckled as they looked on indulgently.

"With a little old driver so lively and quick,

I knew in a moment he must be St. Nick.

More rapid than eagles his coursers they came,

And he whistled, and shouted, and called them by name:

"Now, Dasher! now, Dancer! now Prancer and Vixen!

On, Comet! on, Cupid! on, Donner and Blitzen!

To the top of the porch! to the top of the wall!

Now dash away! dash away! dash away all!"

As leaves that before the wild hurricane fly,

When they meet with an obstacle, mount to the sky;

So up to the housetop the coursers they flew

With the sleigh full of toys, and St. Nicholas too—

And then, in a twinkling, I heard on the roof

The prancing and pawing of each little hoof.

As I drew in my head, and was turning around,

Down the chimney St. Nicholas came with a bound.

He was dressed all in fur, from his head to his foot,

And his clothes were all tarnished with ashes and soot;

A bundle of toys he had flung on his back,

And he looked like a peddler just opening his pack.

His eyes—how they twinkled! his dimples, how merry!

His cheeks were like roses, his nose like a cherry!

His droll little mouth was drawn up like a bow,

And the beard on his chin was as white as the snow;

The stump of a pipe he held tight in his teeth."

Byron waved his pipe dramatically, making the children laugh.

"And the smoke, it encircled his head like a wreath;

He had a broad face and a little round belly

That shook when he laughed, like a bowl full of jelly.

He was chubby and plump, a right jolly old elf,

And I laughed when I saw him, in spite of myself;

A wink of his eye and a twist of his head

Soon gave me to know I had nothing to dread;

He spoke not a word, but went straight to his work,

And filled all the stockings; then turned with a jerk,

And laying his finger aside of his nose,

And giving a nod, up the chimney he rose;

He sprang to his sleigh, to his team gave a whistle,

And away they all flew like the down of a thistle.

But I heard him exclaim, ere he drove out of sight—"

Byron paused and someone else bellowed the final phrase in a deep sonorous voice.

"Happy Christmas to all, and to all a good night!"

The children all squealed in delight as a fully dressed white-bearded St. Nicholas strode into the room.

"Well, hello there!" Byron nodded at Santa Claus.

"Hello! And who do we have here?" Santa Claus peered down at the group of children as he hefted a heavy velvet bag from his shoulder. The children realized now was the time to open presents and they clustered around the Santa as he began to parcel out the gifts to the children.

"Morgan, who plays the Santa?" Brie whispered.

"The groundskeeper, Mr. Grange. He lives for this role every year," Morgan chuckled.

Brie could now see a hint of the groundskeeper beneath the realistic white beard and wig.

"Now, before you go play with your new toys, would you like to meet my reindeer?"

The resounding shouts of "yes" made Santa Claus grin. "This way! This way, little ones!"

"Is he serious?" asked Brie.

"Oh yes," said Morgan.

The adults followed him and the children outside. There on the front of the snow-covered driveway was indeed an ornate sleigh with a team of eight living, breathing reindeer, strapped with bell-covered harnesses.

Brie marveled at the sight. The children were given sugar cubes and took turns feeding the reindeer for several minutes. Then Santa declared he had to leave to visit other children.

"If he makes that thing fly, then I know I'm in a coma at the hospital," Brie said and Morgan chuckled.

Santa climbed into the sleigh and tapped the reindeer with the leather reins. The reindeer pulled the sleigh around the edge of the house and out of sight. Everyone headed back indoors where the children opened their gifts. Lyra got a sketchbook and colored pencil set which she showed to Thad and Veronica, who gave her a thumbs up.

"Julia got an advance Christmas list for all the kids," Morgan explained. "We invite some of our friends who attend the reading each year and mum's brilliant at planning it all out, right down to the gifts."

"That's smart. Some of those younger ones really seem to believe that was Santa Claus." Brie was moved by the look of joy on the children's faces, but she was still all too aware of Alec standing nearby and the way his eyes never left her as he talked to other guests.

By midnight, the children were escorted to bed and the adults without children were finishing their glasses of Merryvale's famous sloe gin before heading to bed themselves. Brie, not currently engaged with anyone, took this opportunity to slip away as well

"Brie." Alec blocked her exit as she tried to leave the drawing room. Her heart gave a jolt at his sudden appearance.

"Alec..." She said his name in a warning tone.

"I have a gift for you."

"No, you shouldn't. That's a bad idea." She shook her head, but he pulled her into his arms before she could protest further. His masculine scent was intoxicating and brought back every wonderful memory she had of him in the last few days.

"Just one." He led her to her bedroom where a large Christmas box with some holes in the side sat on her bed.

"What is it?" she asked. The box suddenly moved a little and a soft noise came from it.

"Oh my God." Brie looked Alec. "What is it?" She repeated. She was not at all reassured by his soft smile. She quickly approached the box and lifted the loose lid. A small furry bundle sat inside the box, wiggling and whining softly, a big red bow tied around its neck. She stared at it. It was a Cocker Spaniel puppy.

"She's for you." Alec came up behind her, his hand encircling her waist as he held her close to him. A dozen emotions ripped through her, sharp and almost violent.

"You said that you love dogs but never really had a chance to have one. She's had all her proper shots and she won't have to wait in quarantine to fly home with you."

Brie picked up the puppy and cradled it in her arms. It nuzzled her throat and its tiny tongue licked her everywhere she could. She couldn't help but giggle.

"Do you like her?"

"Like her? Only a monster wouldn't like her. She's precious. Are you sure I can take her home?" Brie rubbed her cheek against the puppy's silky head. That sweet innocent puppy smell filled her nose and her eyes with tears. This was one of those things she'd missed out on her whole life: the bliss of holding a puppy in her arms. She turned to Alec, whose soft hazel eyes glowed in the gilded light from the chandelier above them.

"I know you want this to be over but give me one last night just to hold you." His voice was soft and slightly raspy as he entreated her with his plea.

"It's not that I don't want to be with you, Alec. We keep saying we're adults, but that doesn't mean things can't get complicated, even if we don't intend for them to."

Alec nodded. "I understand. And it's not like I haven't had those same concerns. It's fair to say that I've grown fond of you in the time we've had together."

"I'm fond of you too."

"So, it must seem like a cold and callous thing to have those kind of feelings, yet agree to end things as well."

"And there's the matter of our jobs and separate lives."

"Yes, I know. But wouldn't you regret it more if we didn't make the most of the time we had?" His hands cupped her shoulders and slid up and down her arms as he waited for a response. She slowly nodded. It was impossible to deny herself what she wanted.

"One more night."

One more night to pretend she could have the life she always wanted. Alec leaned in and pressed his lips to hers. The puppy wriggled for a moment then rested in between the two of them. Alec tangled his fingers in Brie's hair as he kissed her deeply. His mouth slanted over hers and the kiss turned into a slow burn that whispered of dark nights and secretly sinful pleasures. There was a lifetime of dreams and desires passing between them as their mouths danced with one another.

The puppy whined, as if telling them she wanted to play too. They broke apart and laughed. Alec ruffled the puppy's ears.

"You need to name her."

Brie held the puppy up to peer more deeply into the dark pools of her brown eyes.

"She looks like an Ainsley to me."

"Ainsley it is." Alec held open his arms. "She has a kennel already. Want me to put her down for the night?"

"Does she need to eat? Or, you know, go out?"

"No, she's been taken care of by a footman."

"Great." Brie kissed Ainsley's forehead and then passed the pup to Alec, who carried her over to the little kennel and tucked her in before closing the door.

Ainsley whined softly for a moment before settling down.

"Thank you, Alec. She's perfect. I don't know how

she'll adjust to my apartment, but at least I live across from a park." Brie was already picturing her life with the puppy and it made her smile.

"I wanted you to have something special to remember this place...to remember us."

Brie's throat tightened and her smile faltered, but she regained her resolve. It was like he said: she'd regret it more if they didn't make the most of the time they had.

"I can think of another way to remember this." She gripped his sweater and pulled him to her, kissing him hard. She didn't want any more regrets, at least not for one more night.

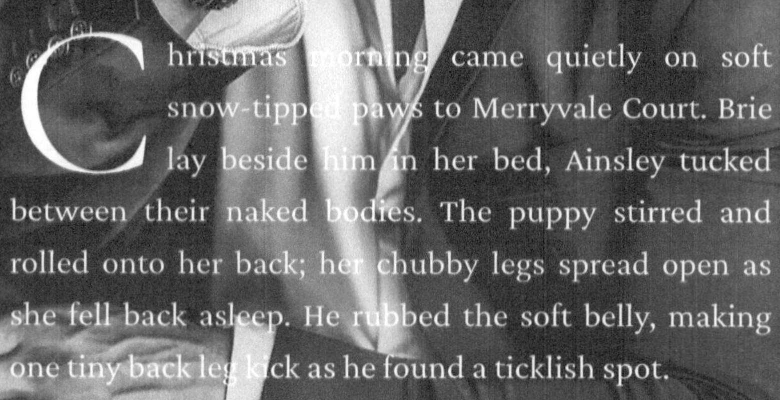

13

Christmas morning came quietly on soft snow-tipped paws to Merryvale Court. Brie lay beside him in her bed, Ainsley tucked between their naked bodies. The puppy stirred and rolled onto her back; her chubby legs spread open as she fell back asleep. He rubbed the soft belly, making one tiny back leg kick as he found a ticklish spot.

"How on earth did you end up here?" he murmured to the dog.

Brie opened one eye to stare at him. "It's my fault." She bit her bottom lip to cover up a grin but failed. "She cried early this morning and I just had to let her out. She wanted to be in bed with us."

"If you spoil her now..."

"I know." Brie groaned. "I'm going to be a terrible dog mom."

"I suppose that's a matter of opinion. I'm sure Ainsley will think you're the best." He scratched his fingers under Ainsley's chin. The puppy sighed and licked her lips in contentment.

"What time is it?" Alec rolled over to check his watch and then flung himself back down on the bed. "The bagpipers will start in a few minutes."

"What? I thought that wasn't until ten?"

"It is nearly ten." He retrieved his Breitling watch from the nightstand to show her.

"Oh God. Your mom must be waiting for me!" Brie threw the covers back and sat up.

"Probably, but you shouldn't worry. Get dressed. I'll have someone take Ainsley out for you."

Brie slid out of bed. "Thanks." Alec folded his arms behind his head as he enjoyed the view of her delectable backside as she bent to pick up her clothes off the floor and put them in her suitcase before retrieving a fresh outfit to wear.

His phone buzzed and he leaned over to grab it from the nightstand. A dozen emails were bolded in his inbox. He groaned. The office was bugging him on Christmas day of all days to start the acquisition paper-work. This was why he hadn't been home for Christmas the last three years. Whoever stayed in London to work on whatever deal was going down always got the bonuses, raises and recognition. It was also far easier to bury himself in work on Christmas day and not think about losing his grandfather.

"What is it?" Brie asked. She was dressed now, her lovely curves half hidden beneath the deep cranberry colored sweater.

"Work. I need to go handle this. If you want to take Ainsley out early, her leash is in her crate."

"I'll take her." Brie pulled on her boots and picked the puppy up. She collected the red leash and carried the dog out of the room. Alec got out of bed and dressed. He'd have to work for a few hours but then he'd be able to enjoy some of the day with Brie and his family.

As he left Brie's room, he thought back to last night and how Brie had been everything he'd wanted. Yet even as she drifted to sleep, he'd seen a flash of something in her eyes. Resignation? Reservation? Some combination of the two?

It shouldn't matter. Last night was simply that. The *last* night. They would both go back to their separate lives. It shouldn't bother him, but it did.

For the next two hours he worked on his laptop in his room, unable to shake the knot of worry in his chest.

He could hear the distant Christmas music and knew everyone was downstairs having fun while he was working. Wasn't that how things were supposed to be? Wasn't that how he'd always wanted it to be?

BRIE SPENT THE FIRST HALF OF THE DAY TAKING PICTURES OF the bagpipers and the Christmas turkey, roasted chutney, and artichoke soup that were served for the main meal. She laughed as everyone popped the brightly colored Christmas crackers and wore the flimsy paper crowns will they shared the jokes from their crackers.

Nearly twenty people filled the massive dining room table, but one seat was empty. Alec's.

Julia and Byron both attempted to pretend the vacant seat didn't exist. It was depressingly clear that they were used to the eldest son not attending Christmas activities. Morgan, on the other hand, was the life of the party. He, and many of the others, wore terrible Christmas sweaters as part of an ugly sweater contest. Yet when he glanced toward Brie, she saw a hint of something in his eyes that warned her his charm was a cover. He looked...disappointed, not that she could guess why.

By early evening, Alec finally come downstairs and

slipped in to join the celebrations. His parents wished him a happy Christmas, but Brie didn't miss their disappointment. Alec moved through the crowds until he was standing next to her. The kids drank hot apple cider while the adults enjoyed various dessert drinks like sherry and port.

"Did you get your work done?" Brie asked.

"Mostly. I'll be busy for a week or so, and then it's another couple weeks until the next big deal comes our way."

Brie didn't reply. In a way she was glad. Her foolish heart had so desperately wanted to connect itself to him, but this was a stark reminder that it would never have worked out. The last few days have been a nice vacation but that's all it was: a vacation.

"So, you leave tomorrow?" Alec asked. "That's Boxing Day. Don't you want to stay for that?"

"I can't." Brie knew she could, but she wasn't going to draw out the goodbyes more than she had to. She had everything she needed for the book. Everything else would be handled over phone and email. She'd come to love Merryvale and the Halston family, and it felt like a knife to her heart when she thought about leaving them.

"Are you and Morgan going back tomorrow?" she asked.

"I'm afraid so." Alec's gaze caught on his brother. "I don't know how he does it. I know his job is complex and demanding, yet he acts like he has all the time in the world."

Brie sighed and ruffled Ainsley's fur. The puppy was tucked between her legs. "He knows what matters. He cares about his family enough to make it his priority." Shock flashed in Alec's eyes. She didn't mean for it to sound accusing, but before she could apologize, Ainsley ran away from her on chubby legs toward the other three dogs and Brie had to chase after her. Ainsley bumped into Yogi and barked at his behemoth body as though it were a bulldog shaped mountain. Brie couldn't help but think Ainsley would be happier here with this family instead of a lonely, tiny apartment.

"Brie, are you okay?" Veronica asked.

"Yeah, I'm fine." She just had to hold herself together one more night and then she would be going home.

"When you get to the airport tomorrow be sure to call me, okay?"

"I will." Brie promised and hugged her.

Brie stepped back into the shadow of the room to better watch the guests at the party. Someone began a rousing chorus of *God Rest Ye Merry Gentlemen*. Byron and Morgan sang it proudly, their voices carrying across the room. Alec stood not too far away, watching them, a hint of sorrow in his eyes. Why didn't he want this? Couldn't he see how amazing his family was?

But Brie knew she couldn't judge Alec. She was the same. Afraid of getting hurt, afraid of making a mistake again. She slipped out of the drawing room and into the hall. A number of guests were milling about or headed up to bed. She smiled and wished them a good night as she climbed the stairs. When she reached the top, she glanced down once more at the shaft of light coming out of the partially open drawing room door.

"Bit much, eh?" someone said.

She turned to see an older man she didn't recognize leaving a room a few feet from the top of the stairs where she stood.

"Yeah, I don't have family anymore and I forgot how intense it can be in a crowded room for a long time. But I love it too."

The man chuckled. "Yes, having the family around is good, even when they are *intense* at times, as you put it. I'm sorry you lost yours."

"Thanks."

The man removed a cigar from his pocket and lit it. He puffed once and the smell was rather pleasant. He was older, in his mid-seventies, with silver hair and kind brown eyes.

"Ah. You must be Julia's writer." The man looked at the notebook she'd been carrying around all day.

"I am."

"What do you think of the place? Be honest now."

"It's lovely. It's not just a fancy country house, and it's not a museum. It's a home. That's the part I want readers to know. Julia, Byron, and their family breathe life into the history of this place. They continue its graceful traditions not out of duty but out of a desire to carry on what is worth loving about this place."

The man puffed on his cigar again. "You sound very wise for one so young."

"Sometimes I don't feel young," she admitted. She was only twenty-nine, but in many ways, she felt ancient. She'd been married, divorced, and lost her parents. It had aged her in a way.

"Only the young *feel* young and they're too young to realize the value in it."

"That's true," Brie agreed. "Are you staying tomorrow with the family?"

"A few more days should do it," the man said. "I never want to miss Christmas at Merryvale. There's no place like it in the world."

"It is magical," she agreed. "Well, it was nice to meet you." She shook his hand.

"Same to you, my dear." The man puffed on his cigar as he headed toward the stairs.

When Brie reached her room, she remembered Ainsley was still downstairs. She dropped her notebook on her bed and glanced at her unpacked suitcase. It was one more thing to do before she left this place.

"You forgot your little companion." Morgan announced from her doorway, holding Ainsley.

"Thank you. I was just coming to get her." She accepted the puppy from his arms and a laugh escaped her as she saw up close how truly atrocious Morgan's sweater was. It was an ugly pastel illustration of a bulbous-nosed Santa.

"Go ahead and laugh." Morgan said. "But, I won."

"Tell me you bought that at a joke store." She laughed again.

"Hardly." He glanced down at the ugly thing. "I bought it at a retail store. The sweater wasn't a joke. At least, not to the shop that sold it." He watched her put Ainsley in the kennel.

"So, you leave tomorrow?" Morgan asked.

"Yes. Back to work, I'm afraid. You?" She folded her arms over her chest.

"Tomorrow as well, but not until the evening." Morgan stepped closer, partly closing the door behind him. "Brie, would you consider staying?"

"Staying?" She eyed him in concern. "I can't, Morgan."

"Please." He reached out and clasped her hands in his.

"Oh Morgan, I'm sorry but I didn't mean to make you think that I was..." She wasn't sure how to tell him she wasn't interested in him, at least not like this. His lips curved into a rueful smile.

"What? Oh, no. Not for me, for Alec. I know you two have a connection."

"What?" A lump formed in her throat. If he knew... what if he told Julia?

"Oh, come now. You'd have to be blind not to see it. There's chemistry between you two." Morgan's smile was gentle and it gave her some small measure of relief.

"You're not upset? I sort of had the impression your mom wanted you and me to get together."

Morgan's eyes twinkled with mischief. "She's a matchmaker, all right. But she knows I won't settle down. Alec though, he's different. With the right person, he can learn to be himself again."

Brie shivered. "I wish I was that person, but I'm not ready to be in a relationship again."

"Are you still in love with your ex?" Morgan asked.

"No, that's not what I meant." Brie sighed and pulled her hands free of his. "I don't trust myself. I want to believe in love, to believe it's real, but I don't trust myself not to make the same mistake again." She looked up at the glass chandelier.

"What does love mean to you?" Morgan asked her.

"I don't know..." She stared at him, wishing she could explain it. "I guess that's my problem isn't it? I don't know it well enough to see it in another person."

"You know, Alec was my grandfather's favorite. Don't get me wrong, Walter loved me, but there was something about Alec that truly made them bond. I've wondered about that, what makes two souls connect, makes them inseparable? It's like on some level you realize being apart from them leaves you feeling cold and alone in a bone deep way. Alec must feel like that whenever he thinks of our grandfather. It's how I feel about my parents. That's why I come home every holiday. I'd rather risk the pain than never know the joy of loving and being loved." Morgan slid his hands into his pockets, a sheepish grin on his face.

"The thing is, for the few days you were here, we saw the old Alec. The person he was before Walter died. You were good for him. Maybe he was good for you too?"

"Maybe," Brie conceded. "But we're talking about the real world here. Sometimes it really is just too complicated."

Morgan thought about that, then nodded. "I'm sorry that it didn't work out."

Brie smiled sadly. "Me too."

Morgan leaned in and pressed a faint kiss to her cheek before he left. Brie stared at Ainsley, now sleeping in her carrier. Brie knew she needed to pack but she came to the sad realization that she couldn't bring anything reminiscent of Alec back with her, it would simply be too much.

IT WAS CLOSE TO MIDNIGHT. ALEC LEFT HIS BEDROOM AND wandered down the hall. He couldn't sleep. His mind kept going over everything that happened these last few days. He was torn, but he shouldn't be. His life was back in London.

He paused at the door of his grandfather's study. The light was still on. He pushed the door open and stepped inside, only to stop dead in his tracks. There was someone sitting at his grandfather's desk, smoking a cigar and clutching a glass of scotch.

"Grandfather?" Alec's voice was faint. He gazed at the form of his very real, very present grandfather.

Walter smiled. "Been a long time, hasn't it, my boy?"

"I… but…you…" Alec stammered.

"Yes." Walter chuckled. "That doesn't mean I've reached the end."

"What do you mean?" Alec couldn't stop staring. This was a dream. It had to be. But it felt so heartbreakingly *real*, right down to the smell of the cigars.

"Do you remember when I used to tell you about that female astronomer from the nineteenth century?"

Alec nodded. "Yes, Lysandra Russell."

"And do you remember what she used to say?" Walter asked.

Throat tight, Alec spoke. "We are all, each of us, made of stardust."

"That's right. Everything on this earth, every atom, every molecule was at one time a part of a cosmic cloud of dust that came from a dying star. When that cosmic dust swirled tight under pressure, new planets and new stars were formed. Nothing that dies ever stays dead, Alec. We are all stardust."

"This has to be a dream," Alec muttered. "But I've dreamt about you before and it's never felt like this."

"It's because you're *here*," Walter said. "You've been running away from home a long time. I couldn't find you, not until you came back."

"I came home a few years ago for the holidays." Alec argued.

Walter's eyes were heavy. "You came to Merryvale, but you left your heart in London, locked away from all those who love you. This time it's different. *You're* different."

"How?" Alec asked. But he already knew the answer. "Brie..."

"Now you're starting to see, my boy." His grandfather pushed his chair back and stood.

"Grandfather..." Alec spoke again, fearing the dream wouldn't last. All dreams had to end, didn't they?

"Yes?"

"I'm sorry I didn't come home sooner, but I was afraid."

"It's all right to be afraid. What matters is what you do in the face of it." Walter came over and placed a hand on Alec's shoulder for a moment before he walked past him toward the door. Alec spun to say something, but no one was there. The light in the room faded from gold to moonlit shadows.

Alec shivered and realized he must have been sleep-walking. He inhaled deeply. Walter's cigar smoke still filled the air. Alec rubbed his arms and walked back to his room, more confused than ever. What did it mean? What was he meant to do? And was he brave enough once he knew the answer?

14

Goodbyes were never easy for Brie. She wiped away tears as she hugged Byron and Julia. Morgan, Thad, Veronica, and Lyra were all there as well. Alec, however, was noticeably absent. Morgan had said something about him being caught up in work in his room. She doubted that was entirely true, but perhaps it was for the best. She wasn't sure she could face him. It would hurt too much to say goodbye to him for a second time.

"I'm so glad you don't mind me leaving Ainsley here. She seems so happy with the other dogs." Brie watched the puppy running around Morgan's legs, yipping in delight as Yogi trundled after her, enjoying the game of chase.

"Of course," Byron said. "Merryvale can never have too many dogs. Are you sure you won't reconsider?"

"I wish I could. But she would be unhappy in my tiny apartment."

"Well, you can come visit her when the book is published. I will insist upon that," Julia said, even though she'd already spent the last hour during breakfast reminding Brie that she could visit as often as she wished. As they hugged, Julia continued, "You're part of our family now."

Brie wished that were true. It would be an honor to be part of their family.

"Thank you so much for opening your home to me." Brie's throat tightened as she struggled to keep a smile in place.

Julia hugged her again. "Of course, my dear. There are so many things I want to thank you for, but now isn't the time. I don't want you to miss your flight."

Brie got into the SUV that would take her to Manchester and cast one last look out the windows at a place that had come to feel like home in so short a time. It wasn't just the ancient stones and trees, or the sloping snowy hills, or that the place looked like it belonged in a fairy tale. It was the people within the house's walls that had stolen her heart. Byron with his quiet confidence. Julia with her open heart. Morgan and his good-natured charm.

But above all else, she would miss Alec. She would miss the way he touched her, the way he kissed her as though he had all the time in the world yet couldn't get enough of her. She would miss how they talked late into the night and how it felt to simply *be* while she was near him. But she also feared what it would be like to stay, to try again to chase after what she thought she had with Preston.

Why was she so afraid? Brie wished she knew the answer. Looking into the darkest parts of her soul, at her own fears and failings, was something no one liked to do. She'd avoided it for a long time.

But as she boarded the plane in Manchester that day, she finally faced the truth: she was afraid. Afraid to find love. Afraid it *would* be real and even more afraid she would screw it up somehow. Perhaps meeting Alec had been the universe telling her that she could still have a chance, maybe not with him but with someone else.

By the time Brie landed in Chicago fifteen hours later, she found herself outside baggage claim with nothing to do but wait for the parade of luggage to begin.

She pulled up some social media apps on her phone and searched for Preston. She gasped when she found him. He was hugging a lovely woman and holding the hand of a child who looked to be about two years old.

The pain she expected didn't come, only a poignant bittersweet ache. He had what she wanted. He'd managed to find it after their shared life had crumbled down around them. It gave her hope, like a field of early blooming wildflowers, defiant against the cold late winter winds.

She pulled up her contacts and found Preston's number and after moment's hesitation, dialed it. It was possible he'd changed his number, but she wanted to try. It rang only once before he answered.

"Brie?" He sounded surprised, but not upset.

"Hey Preston," she said softly. "I probably shouldn't have called you, but I need to talk for a minute. Is that okay?"

"Hey, of course," Preston said. He sounded different. More engaged, more...something she couldn't quite define.

"I saw that you remarried. You have a son?"

"Yeah, I do." Preston's warm chuckle brought back happy memories. "His name is Jake. My wife is Izzy."

"Congratulations." Brie meant it. She'd never wished him ill, and she knew he hadn't wished her ill either.

"So, what did you want to talk about?"

Brie summoned her courage and hoped this wasn't a mistake. "Well...how did you do it? I mean, fall in love again? How did you know it was real this time?"

God, she must sound crazy and pathetic. There was a long pause, but he didn't end the call. He drew in a deep breath and then spoke.

"It didn't happen overnight, I can tell you that." He hesitated. "You know...I kept tabs on you after the first year," Preston said quietly. "I thought I should walk away clean, but we were friends. I worried about you."

That stunned her. Preston had cared after all that? She swallowed thickly.

"But I was worried you hated me, and I didn't want to make things worse. I'm sorry. Looking back, I think we could have done each other a lot of good if we'd just talked more. It would have saved us a lot of time."

"Maybe you're right. I'm sorry too."

"So, you're wondering what changed since then?"

"Yeah."

"Well, for the first year after we got divorced, I

buried myself in work. You know how I was. Then I realized I was getting by fine from day to day, but looking back on that year? I hadn't lived at all. I realized that life wasn't working out any better than our marriage. It was just another holding pattern."

Brie could relate to that.

"Then I was getting coffee one morning and I saw this woman in a shop, reading a fat book by some old Russian guy and I couldn't help but laugh. She reminded me of you," Preston said this fondly.

"Anyway, she sees me clearly laughing at her and calls me out on it, which also reminded me of you. I apologized and introduced myself. I told her why I was laughing and rather than be offended she laughed as well, like she got it, like she got *me*. Turns out she's a professor of English lit at the University of Columbia."

"Wow…" Brie could never imagine Preston settling down with another bookworm, but she was glad.

"So, we went out for coffee, then dinner, then movies. We took it slow. I was gun shy about getting married again, but one morning I woke up and realized that if I had to go a day without her in my life it would hurt like hell. I couldn't stand to think about it. I proposed to her then and there, with no ring or anything. I'm still surprised she said yes." Preston laughed again. "We got married and then Jake came along. He's barely two. I left my job after we got married. Now I run a small regional bank as a CFO. Great benefits, excellent daycare, and simple nine to five work hours. Haven't worked a day of overtime all year. I never imagined I would want any of that four years ago, but it's all that matters now. Funny how life is, isn't it?"

"It really is." Brie thought back to the moment she'd first seen Alec, and how he turned out so different, so much more complex and wonderful than she ever could have dreamed.

"So, how about you? Is everything okay with you?"

"I'm okay, really. I've got an amazing job as a ghost-writer." She mentioned a few of her better-known books.

"Believe it or not, we have a few of those on the shelves here at the house. I'll have to tell Izzy. She would love to know a famous author." Brie heard only genuine sincerity in his voice. "Brie, why did you really call? I mean, don't get me wrong, I'm really glad you did, but why?"

Preston had been so open and honest with her that she didn't want to close up on him now.

"I met someone. He was a lot like you. Funny how that is." She drew in a deep breath. "I felt things for him, but I was afraid that given what happened with us it would happen all over again. I...I think I made another mistake."

"That's good it, isn't it?" Preston answered softly. "Life is about making mistakes. Not all mistakes are the end of the road. Sometimes they keep us on the right path. Call it failing forward. Don't give up. I think you and I were practicing. I know that sounds ridiculous, but I don't regret one minute of being married to you, Brie." His voice softened. "You deserve to be happy and to have a life you've always dreamed of. Just let go of your fear and give it another chance. And even if turns out to be a mistake, try again. Fail forward."

Brie's throat tightened and, for moment, she couldn't make a sound. Finally, she managed to suck in a breath. "Thank you, Preston. That means more than you know."

"Hey, I mean it," Preston insisted. "If you ever need me, call me. Izzy would love to meet you."

"That might be fun. I'll think about it." Brie promised and she meant it. For some reason the thought of meeting Preston's wife didn't sound as painful as she might've imagined.

"Well, it's almost dinner so I've got some mac & cheese to make for my little man. It's bachelor night for Jake and me. Izzy's at a work thing." He laughed.

"Sounds like fun." Brie smiled. "Take care, Preston."

"You too, Brie."

Brie ended the call and stared at the phone, her breath coming more deeply now. Tears blurred her eyes, but she felt free. It was as though she'd been trapped in a dark cave her whole life and was only now glimpsing the bright beautiful world around her. Even the rushing chaos at the Newark airport and the march of unclaimed luggage around the carousel seemed beautiful.

Was this what it was like to face one's fears and learn you were strong enough to keep going forward? If it was, she could do it. Maybe love would truly find her this time.

ALEC HEADED DOWNSTAIRS AFTER FINISHING THE LAST DETAILS of his acquisition. He'd worked twice as hard early this morning, but the time had still gotten away from him. He found everyone having a light lunch in the dining room.

"Alec, you came down finally." Morgan observed that his usual smile looked forced.

"What's the matter?" He saw more than one gloomy face amongst the crowd.

"What's the *matter*?" Morgan asked. "Where the bloody hell were you three hours ago?"

"What happened three hours ago?" The pit of dread filled his stomach like lead.

"Brie's gone." Thad said.

Alec checked his watch, his heart lurching into his throat. "But I thought she didn't leave until two."

"That was her London flight," Veronica said. "She left for Manchester this morning."

"Why didn't you come to get me?" Alec demanded.

Morgan stood, scowling as he crossed his arms. "Why? I can't do everything for you Alec. If you cared enough about her you would've figured that out and been down here."

Alec stared in open disbelief. He'd never seen his brother like this.

"Morgan..."

"No." His brother waved a hand to silence him. "You've made a right mess of things. We've all worked so hard to help you and Brie end up together. You just let her slip away. I'm done helping."

"Wait." Alec stared at all the red flush faces around the room. "What's that supposed to mean? You all arranged this?"

Morgan glared at him but said nothing. His mother

cleared her throat. "Well…we knew you wouldn't come here unless Thad invited you."

Thad waved his hand in acknowledgment.

"Veronica had a feeling that you might like Brie, so she helped arrange for Brie to come…"

Alec's temper was starting to build. He didn't like being played with like some fool. "But you all kept talking about trying to set up Brie with Morgan."

"A bit of sibling rivalry goes a long way with you two," his father pointed out.

"But you couldn't have known I'd met her before I arrived." He realized too late he given away what seemed to be his last secret.

"Of course, we did." His mother scoffed. "I called your executive assistant at Barclays a few months ago and got your flight and seat information. It was only too easy to book Brie next to you." His mother's voice trembled now. "I never dreamed the second flight would crash, though."

"We didn't crash. It was an emergency landing!" Alec nearly snapped. Why he was nitpicking he had no idea.

"Well, you sure crashed this." Morgan started to leave the room, but he stopped next to Alec. "Brie's a good woman. The two of you clicked. Everyone could see it. And you just let her slip away. I mean, is work really *that* important to you? Why don't you settle down for Christ's sake?"

"Why don't you?" Alec shot back.

Morgan's gave a rueful smile. A hint of bitterness lingered in his gaze.

"I almost did, once. But I missed my chance. At least you still have time left to go after her."

"You're all mad. Brie is a wonderful woman, yes, but we barely know each other. A handful of days isn't enough time."

"But you'll never find someone if you don't *take* the time," Thad countered. "And maybe, if you're brave enough, you'll see what's been right before your eyes all along."

Alec felt betrayed. His family had conspired to set him up with Brie. But by not telling either of them, Alec and Brie had treated their time together in the only logical way: a passing rendezvous. She'd said she didn't want any relationships, and neither had he.

And the arrogance of them assuming they'd be a good fit. What if he'd hated her? What if she'd hated him? What kind of meddling had they planned to help them like each other? Did they have any idea how disastrous this could have turned out? Only a few times in his life had he been set up to fail, and it was not something he liked to experience again.

"I need to leave," he muttered and exited the room. His family stayed behind, silently watching him. At the bottom of the stairs, he felt something tug at his boots. He glanced down and saw Ainsley pulling at his jeans. She stopped, released his pantleg and looked up, wagging her tail.

She hadn't taken the puppy. She'd left *his* gift behind. He sank to his knees and lifted the puppy into his arms, clutching her to his chest as he fought off the rolling wave of grief he felt at losing her.

"How could she leave you?" he asked Ainsley. The dog licked his ear and snuggled into his arms. "Well, *I* won't leave you. You're coming with me."

He stood and carried the puppy to his bedroom so he could pack. He was leaving for London immediately. It would give him time away from his family. Time to think.

ALEC CARRIED AINSLEY INSIDE AN EXPENSIVE BLACK ANIMAL shoulder strap case as he walked into his office. The puppy had both a large breakfast and a good walk and he was pretty confident she would not make too much of a fuss while he worked at the office for a few hours. He'd brought a pee pad folded up in his attaché case for emergencies though. In the last few days he'd gotten rather good at living with the adorable little scamp in his London flat.

The teetering stacks of letters he found in his office inbox tray made him groan. He set the dog carrier down and closed the door. He checked on Ainsley, who was still sleeping. He opened the side of the carrier to let her come out and explore when she was ready. He was nearly done going through the letters when someone knocked on his door.

"Enter," he called out. When he realized it was Mr. Eppley, he hastily got to his feet. Ainsley stirred from her carrier and peeked her head out.

Howard, ever with a sharp eye, noticed the visitor immediately. "Brought someone to work, eh?" He bent down to better examine the cocker spaniel puppy as she toddled out of the carrier to sniff his shoes. Her little ball of a tail wiggled the entire time.

"She was an unexpected Christmas gift from my brother."

Howard chuckled. "You know someone pities you when they buy you a dog. But dogs are good for a man's soul. I had a borzoi when I was younger man. Beautiful dog. I always think of what that writer John Galsworthy said about them."

"Oh?" Alec watched as Ainsley took an experimental nibble of one of the laces on Howard's patent leather shoes.

"*'Not the least hard thing to bear when they go from us, these quiet friends, is that they carry away with them so many years of our own lives.'*"

Alec didn't want to think about what Ainsley might someday carry away with her when she passed on. Already the dog had claimed at least one amazing night where Alec had held Brie in his arms. He wouldn't trade that memory for anything, and Ainsley had been a part of it.

"Well, the reason I came here was to congratulate you. The clients were very pleased. As you can imagine there's talk of promotions." Howard grinned. "You've also got Montgomery on the run. He's been fuming all week about how you pulled it off while taking it easy in the country."

Alec wasn't sure where Howard was headed. This didn't sound like your average attaboy moment.

"Point is, Halston, *now* is the time for big decisions."

Alec released a weary breath. "I feared you might say that."

"Don't sound so downbeat. The company is ready to offer you my job. I've been promoted to president of investments for the entire UK."

"Congratulations, Mr. Eppley."

Howard waved a hand. "So, it seems you have a choice, Halston. You can take my job, it's a surefire track to the top or…"

"Or I reconsider my employment options." They both knew that staying in his current position wasn't going to be possible, he'd suffer burnout in a few years.

Alec retrieved a letter from his desk. He hesitated, not because he wasn't sure of his decision. He was. But he needed a moment to reflect on the job he had here and what it cost him over the years.

"Here." He placed the letter in Howard's hand. "According to my employment contract, this is one week's notice. But I don't currently have any projects that can't be handled by someone else. I can leave in an hour if you wish."

Howard turned the letter in his hand slowly. He looked at Alec, a hint of amusement in his eyes. "Am I to assume you've had a change of heart about your path after going home for Christmas?"

Alec bent to lift Ainsley up before she could damage Howard's shoes with her sharp puppy teeth. "I have. I was reminded just how important home was, and how much I'd missed staying away from it."

Howard held out his hand. "You're a better man than me. I wish you the best."

Alec shook it. "Thank you, sir." Howard ruffled Ainsley's ear before he turned and walked out the door.

"Time to pack again, little one." Alec set puppy down and began to collect a decade of his life into a cardboard box.

But rather than feeling regret, hope stirred inside him. If there was still time, he had one last thing to collect before going home to Merryvale.

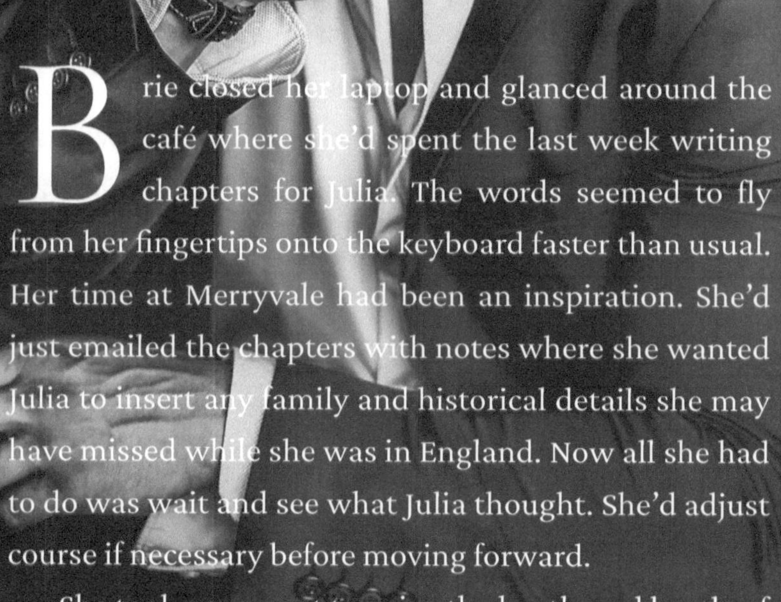

15

Brie closed her laptop and glanced around the café where she'd spent the last week writing chapters for Julia. The words seemed to fly from her fingertips onto the keyboard faster than usual. Her time at Merryvale had been an inspiration. She'd just emailed the chapters with notes where she wanted Julia to insert any family and historical details she may have missed while she was in England. Now all she had to do was wait and see what Julia thought. She'd adjust course if necessary before moving forward.

She took a moment to enjoy the hustle and bustle of the people in the coffee shop while she sipped her peppermint hot chocolate. Soon, thoughts of Alec tiptoed back into her mind. It had been hard trying not to think about him in the last week, but she had. A lot.

After her call to Preston and finding the courage to try again, she'd mentally let the universe know she was open to a second chance at love. She needed to at least be open to whatever possibilities may come her way.

Brie tucked her laptop in her leather messenger bag and slung it over her shoulder before she downed the last bit of hot cocoa. The peppermint still lingered upon her lips as she stepped out into the night. Snow fell in frothy flakes like frozen seafoam on the winter wind. The white light from the park streetlamps across from her apartment had halos of frosted air about them and reminded her of the Snow Queen's kingdom.

With a deep breath, Brie crossed the snowy park back toward her home. She could just make out the shapes of other people walking in the snow through the park. They were like shadows, their voices muffled. Suddenly something small and dark bounded toward her through the snow. She jolted as it barreled into her legs and when she knelt, she gasped. A chocolate colored cocker spaniel puppy stared at her with her little bob of a tail wiggling furiously.

"You are so adorable! You look just like a puppy I used to know. Where's your owner?" She clutched the dog to her chest and stood, frantically searching the snowy ground for whoever had brought her here.

That was when she saw him.

Alec stood ten feet away, a leash in his hand, snow catching in his hair. He and Ainsley were here. Suddenly, all she could think about were those times he'd looked at her with his seductive hazel eyes and how she'd wanted to melt in his arms.

Her heart pounded wildly as they both started to walk toward each other at the same instant. "Alec? What are you doing here?" She nuzzled her face in Ainsley's fur, needing a reminder that this was really happening. That sweet puppy scent was still there, and it brought back memories of the night they'd shared Alec's bed, and how she'd woken up next to Alec with Ainsley wedged between them.

"You left before I could say goodbye," Alec said.

"You came all this way just say goodbye?" She tried to smile, to tease him, but she knew he heard the deeper question in her words.

"I came because letting you walk away was like losing my grandfather all over again. It was like I was losing my *home*." He reached out to touch her cheek and Brie held her breath.

"What about work? Don't you have to go back soon?" She knew this had to be a short trip for work. Just to finish things between them. He couldn't stay. His life was in England.

"I quit. Gave my notice, bought a plane ticket, and came straight here."

"You did *what*? Alec, that wasn't a good idea. You love that job."

He shook his head. "No, I was good at it. I never loved it. It was just a way to escape the pain of being at home and missing my grandfather. But spending Christmas with you changed everything. I realized I wasn't living my life. I was avoiding it." His sensual mouth curved into a devastating smile. "This is me making the grandest gesture I know. Ainsley and I will stay here with you, if you'll have us."

Brie was silent a long moment, her heart soaring though she was so afraid. "Alec...I know what I said before, about love. But I don't feel that way anymore. I want love. I want to do all those silly things that lovers do. I want to get married to someone who I love wildly, who loves me back the same way. I want to have kids and go on adventures with my family. I want to live my life with those I love. I want all of it." There, she'd said it. She'd poured her heart out and now she had to see what happened next.

Alec drew closer, curling his arm around her as he pressed his forehead to hers.

"I want that too. All of it. *With you.*" His warm breath teased her skin and she shivered in his arms.

"You're sure?"

"I've never been more certain of anything in my life." He moved his mouth closer to hers. "Say yes,"

"To what?"

"To everything, to *me.*"

"Yes," Brie said without hesitation.

The kiss that followed belonged to them alone. It was something that Brie would forever try to describe but never quite find the right words.

It was a kiss of endless promises. A kiss of infinite softness. A kiss of fiery heat. It tasted of bittersweet longing and passionate hope. No, that wasn't right. It was all that, yes, but it was something more. Then it came to her.

It was like walking across the lawn toward one's own door. That quiet sense of relief and joy of knowing you were home. It tasted of love, real, pure love that stood defiant against all odds. Every pain she'd endured in the last two weeks had proven at this moment that her feelings for Alec hadn't been lust alone.

What she felt for Alec was real and it always had been.

"I'm home," Alec said.

Brie smiled. "So am I." She cradled Ainsley in her arms and Alec held them both. The snow continued to drift lazily down around them.

Maybe Merryvale's magic was real after all. For an instant, she thought she smelled a hint of cigar smoke on the wind before wintry pine and cedar trees mixed with the snow. Brie's lips curved as she pulled Alec down for another kiss.

EPILOGUE
SIX MONTHS LATER...

Brie lay on a large blanket beneath the towering cedar trees, laughing as Ainsley sprinted after Yogi on the bright green lawns of Merryvale Court.

"Stop! You little thief!" Morgan was chasing after Yogi as well. The bulldog had a large turkey leg in his mouth. Ainsley caught up to Yogi and tried to pull the turkey from his mouth, but almost certainly had no intention of giving it back to Morgan.

"This is why we rarely do picnics on the lawn." Alec chuckled, his rumbling laugh rolling through her where she lay with her head on his chest. They were enjoying the summer weather together and everything was perfect. Brie couldn't have imagined the word "perfect" ever being applied to her life. Yet here it was, all around her. *Perfect.*

"Are you glad we moved here?" Alec asked softly as he ran his fingertips through her hair. It felt amazing. She never wanted him to stop.

"Yes. You?"

He laughed again. "Of course. It's my home."

Alec had lived with her in Chicago for four months before she'd agreed to move to Merryvale with him. It had been surprisingly easy to walk away from her life in the states. Her publishing house kept her on and she worked remotely on all of her writing projects now.

Alec had taken a position at a local bank half an hour away from Merryvale. He'd gotten the idea after Brie told him about her conversation with Preston. He planned to retire from the bank when his father was older and needed more help around the estate.

It had been rather easy settling here, far easier than she could have dreamed. Brie ran her fingertips along Alec's chest before sliding up his body to kiss him. He opened his mouth for her. For a long while, she was lost in just kissing him and how she felt whole with him.

"Wait!" Morgan bellowed a second before Yogi and Ainsley barreled into them on their private blanket paradise.

They broke apart, laughing as Yogi abandoned his

turkey leg and took off running with surprising speed toward the house. Morgan bent over, hands on his knees as he tried to catch his breath while Ainsley claimed her prize.

"You two coming inside, or do you plan to keep snogging like a couple of teenagers?"

"Snogging, definitely," Alec replied before he rolled a laughing Brie beneath him. Morgan rolled his eyes and left.

Brie surrendered to his kisses for a long moment, that may have actually been hours, before they finally broke apart. Alec sighed.

"I suppose we do need to go inside."

"Yes, we do," Brie agreed. "We're getting married tomorrow. I don't want your mother to worry about any last-minute details."

Alec helped her up and they walked hand-in-hand into the house. "Oh, there's no stopping that, I assure you."

"There you are!" Julia exclaimed as she rushed toward them.

"See?" Alec said. "Something the matter, mum?"

"No, something *wonderful* has happened. The books are here!" Julia held up a copy of *Merryvale Christmas: Tales and Traditions* by the Countess of Merryvale and Brie Honeyweather.

Brie accepted the book and skimmed the pages. Her photos, along with the stories and recipes of the Halston family filled the pages in a colorful and engaging way. And this time, her name was there on the cover for all to see. She was no longer a ghostwriter hiding in the shadows.

"Well done, mum." Alec kissed his mother's cheek, then pulled Brie into his embrace and kissed her as well. "Well done to you, too. I hear you had a little something to do with it."

Brie bit her lip and elbowed him in the gut. "I'm on the cover, you jerk."

"So, I see," Alec gasped as he clutched his stomach in feigned pain.

"Brie, dear, if you have a moment..." It didn't take a mind reader to see what Julia wanted to talk to her about.

"Go and talk with mum about the wedding. I'll be just a moment."

"Okay." Brie pulled his shirt collar, so he bent to kiss her again, this one long and deliciously lingering, before she watched him walk away. Her heart swelled, filling her once weary and broken soul with endless love.

❄

ALEC STEPPED INTO HIS GRANDFATHER'S STUDY AND PLACED the last of Walter's old journals down on the desk. He'd spent the last month reading everything he could find from his grandfather. There'd been close to a hundred journals cataloging Walter's life.

Alec eased down into the leather chair. A hint of that old cigar smoke still lingered in the air, but the memory of a ghost was now welcome to him. Coming home to Merryvale had meant finding his grandfather and positive memories in every nook and cranny of the old estate.

Alec removed a new empty leather journal from its packaging and set it down beside his grandfather's on the desk. When he took up a pen and turned to the first page, he thought of his grandfather's stories, the things he learned, and what falling in love with Brie had meant to him.

With a deep breath, he dated the first page and began to write.

Brie and I lay beneath the ancient cedar trees of our home, marveling at the distant striations of clouds as we held each other close, and in that moment, we were infinite...

ABOUT THE AUTHOR

Lauren Smith is an Oklahoma attorney by day, author by night who pens adventurous and edgy romance stories by the light of her smart phone flashlight app. She knew she was destined to be a romance writer when she attempted to re-write the entire *Titanic* movie just to save Jack from drowning. Connecting with readers by writing emotionally moving, realistic and sexy romances no matter what time period is her passion. She's won multiple awards in several romance subgenres including:

New England Reader's Choice Awards, Greater Detroit BookSeller's Best Awards, and a Semi-Finalist award for the Mary Wollstonecraft Shelley Award.

To Connect with Lauren, visit her at:

www.laurensmithbooks.com

lauren@laurensmithbooks.com

facebook.com/LaurenDianaSmith

x.com/LSmithAuthor

instagram.com/Laurensmithbooks